Foxtales 6

by

The Fox Valley Writers' Group:

Nik V. Markevicius

Marie Otte

Ric Waters

John Wesser

Dolores Whitt Becker

Astrid E. L.

Nicole Tolman

Kerry White

Direct all inquiries to:
Facilitator, Fox Valley Writers
foxvalleywriters@gmail.com

Contents

Foreword

One of the great privileges of leading a writers' group is watching the seeds of imagination sprout, grow, and flourish. Each year when I assemble this *Foxtales* anthology, I marvel at the works of literary art occupying the pages. In many instances, I was present at one of our group's meetings when the author drafted a poem, story, or essay in response to a writing prompt. Later, like everyone else involved in the making of the book, I critiqued a more polished version of the work. Finally, when I receive the finished manuscript, I find myself smiling at the way the tale has matured. It's a lot like watching a close friend's kiddos grow; I'm not present every day like a parent, so it's easier to mark the changes and developments of the story.

Each of the authors represented in the following pages has committed significant energy not just to their own work, but that of the group as a whole. The Fox Valley Writers' Group prides itself on supporting and nurturing each other. This edition of *Foxtales,* like those before and those which will come after, represents our passion for both craft and creative community. On behalf of all of us, thank you for choosing to spend your leisure time with this book. I'm certain you won't be disappointed.

Yours truly,

Nik V. Markevicius
Facilitator,
Fox Valley Writers' Group

Nik V. Markevicius

Nik V. Markevicius is that weirdo who's always talking and writing about the bizarre, the off-beat, and the downright strange little what-ifs most people dismiss out of hand. As a non-certified lunatic, he not only listens to the little voices in his head, he argues with them.

Nik is the author of 8 novels and counting, a collection of flash fiction entitled Thong-Sized Stories, *the novella* Head, *numerous short stories, and the* Enchanted Forest State Forest *tales. He is also the current overlord/facilitator of the Fox Valley Writers' Group. Find his work on Amazon.com, inflate your imagination at* theimaginaryplaground.com.

Exit Interview

My boss had me spread out across his desk. It was better than getting bent over it, but not by much. My entire career was laid out in categories, stack by stack on the huge old mahogany desk ahead of his bulging belly.

A thought broke through the greasy low-grade agony of my hangover: *He's bureaucratizing me.* My eyes roved around the desk with each throbbing pulse in my head: reports from me on green carbon copies in one pile to his left; reports about me on yellow carbons next to that; a tall stack of narrow white Vehicle Incident & Repair tags, the kind with copies for me, my boss, this office, the guy doing the work, his boss, and an extra in case the truck had to be sent out to the wider world for greater issues. A lot of body shop letterhead was stapled to those tags.

In a second line before this bureaucrat were my pink discipline reports in another tall stack, yearly performance reviews going back to 1999, and a thin sheaf covered with a page bearing the Illinois State Police logo. My rap sheet, I supposed; nothing there but drunk-and-disorderly, resisting arrest, disturbing the peace, and a single weapons-related technicality where I got shackled for illegal carry on the way to renew my expired firearm owner's ID card. The last stack was taller than all the rest put together. Mostly it was white daily reports, but every so often a couple tangerine pages created a sense of tiger striping. I smiled, thinking of earning those sheets for exceptional performance of duties, assigned or not.

"You're proud of those, aren't you?" asked the bureaucrat, whose measured voice belied the name Frank Yehl. He wore a heavy graying mustache suited to old-school Chicago police, which made his suit look cheap no matter how much he paid for it. I looked from my life-on-paper to him, keeping my smile intact because midlevel managers hate smiles in "serious" meetings like an exit interview. It confuses the shit out of them, since they believe every nuance of their business can and should be *controlled*. When somebody smiles, they suspect subterfuge. After all, false fronts, bullshit, and backstabbing were as much a part of Illinois politics as Abraham Lincoln.

When Yehl's eyes narrowed, I said, "Damn right I am."

He frowned, and with the mustache, it made him look intimidating. He was the kind of big guy who was probably a football linebacker in high school, solid and lean, but he'd expanded until he just barely fit behind his huge antique desk. I'm sure he spent time every morning bunching and relaxing those thick eyebrows so he'd be ready for a good glare. His gleaming bald head only made that face more prominent, until it passed the point of rationality, like a cartoon.

I laughed.

Yehl's bulging eyes almost popped out of his head. "This is funny to you?"

"You bet." I leaned back in my chair and gave him my hardest stare, just to show him what a true tough-guy expression looked like.

He got hold of himself by degrees as the clock on the wall behind me ticked along. I'd been summoned for a ten o'clock meeting, made to wait an hour and a half, and now this bastard wanted to play power-trip games. Since this was my swan song, I didn't think twice before opening my mouth again.

"Can you just get on with it?"

Yehl's upper lip curled into a snarl before he caught himself. His eyes closed. He took a long breath, in-and-out through the nose. When he looked at me again, those eyes seemed to say, *Nice try.*

Yehl folded his hands over the stacks of my life. "Tell me your version of the events of July the seventeenth."

My version... The baiting and goading went both ways. Behind and to the right of the director was a low cabinet full of expensive liquor and sparkling glasses. Half of me considered getting up and fixing myself an uninvited cocktail. The other half thought about drawing my Colt and putting a bullet through the glass front, just to see if Yehl was keyed-up enough to piss his pants.

A tiny third party in my skull suggested I could get hammered in peace, just as soon as this was over.

"Well?" asked the director.

I leaned back in his guest chair and kicked my filthy hiking boots onto the open left corner of his desk. Before Yehl could do more than suck air between his teeth, I started talking.

"I knew something was up when I saw all the mud tracks on Gordon Road after that big storm. That's the road on the southern border of the park-"

"Yes, I know."

"Okay, so, I'm out there, just checking things out, and it's usually pretty quiet because that's the hunting grounds, and it's off-season. So when I see tire treads all over the road by this one entrance, I think, 'Huh.'"

"'Huh?'"

"Y'know, as in, that's weird."

"But you didn't investigate."

"It was lunchtime."

"Ah. So you went to the local bar rather than investigate straightaway, where you proceeded to spend the next two and a half hours drinking in uniform."

I felt my face hardening. "Do you want it *in my own words* or not?"

Another overwrought frown from the director reminded me why I didn't want any part of upper management: nobody got to the goddamn point. They were too busy glaring and harrumphing and folding their arms while they blew air through their bad mustaches.

"Continue."

"So, yeah, I take a long lunch since I'm on-duty from sunrise to sunset whenever another ranger is on vacation, and like you said, I had a couple beers with a burger. That's how I wound up in the bathroom right before I left. While I'm on the can, these two dudes come in and start doing a drug deal.

"There's only one stall, and it's got the handicapped door that shuts by itself, so I guess they didn't realize I was there. That, or they were so used to their routine, they'd gotten sloppy. Whatever. I *was* in there, and one guy says, 'How'd you get here so fast?' and the other one goes, 'This forest has a lot of great hiding spots.'

8

"The first guy goes, 'Got my stuff?' The dealer says, 'If you've got my cash.' They do a deal, they make a minimal bit of small talk, and then leave one at a time."

"And this happened despite the presence of a Ranger's vehicle outside the bar?" asked Yehl.

I took my feet off the desk. The heels thumped the hardwood, and my boss jumped in his seat as I leaned forward. "Cut the bullshit. You know damn well I wasn't in that twenty year-old, no-A/C pickup that can barely climb hills in the winter. I use my own truck."

The director's face turned red, but he held it together. Barely. He twirled his hand in a *go-on* gesture.

"I wipe and flush, then go out to the bartender and ask where the guys are who just came out of the can. He says they left, one at a time, and he lets on that they'd been getting together in his bathroom a couple times a week for at least a month.

"I head outside, and sure enough, there's an SUV leaving the way I'd come in, old and muddy as hell, like it's been off-road more than on. It's painted up in camouflage colors, a real badass custom job that probably costs about what I make in a month. Big loud sucker, too. I hear a lot like that when hunting's on, and I think to myself, *This guy would blend right in.* Then he's gone around the bend, and I'm looking at a beat-up Oldsmobile parked where the willow branches hang down and hide the back end of the lot. I spot a puff of smoke rolling out the window. The breeze pushes it my way, and a second later the smell of cat piss hits my nose.

"I'm sure you know about the meth problems we've had." I tapped the tall stack of reports and commendations. "And you damn well know how I feel about it, if you've bothered to read these."

Yehl scowled some more. Seconds ticked by before he allowed a nod so stiff it must've cost him a chunk of his soul.

I kept leaning over his desk as I went on. "So I did what I always do, which *works,* no matter what you or anybody else thinks of my methods. I hustled over to that Olds and got in on the passenger side.

"This scumbag's behind the wheel. He's got a glass pipe to his lips for another hit. His head whips sideways when I sit down, and when he sees my uniform, his jaw drops. The pipe bounces off the seat between his legs, then thunks when it hits the floor mat. He turns all pasty as the shock of a worst-case-scenario hits him." I grunted a bitter laugh. "Come to think if it, that's the same look my ex-wife had when I caught her boffing the governor. Y'know, when he was still just the comptroller?"

Yehl tried hard for polite disinterest, but his upper lip twitched, and his eyes betrayed the gleaming hunger of a gossip-monger.

I smiled inside and continued, "So, it only lasts a second before he panics and pops the door. I yank him back by the hair, and what's he do? He spins back and comes at me with fists flailing. Dumbass idea in close quarters. He clunked the windshield with his left hand and popped a knuckle on the right when a ring snagged a rip in his headrest. Before he can adjust, I headbutt him. His eyes cross and he goes all limp, and the next thing he knows I've got my knife pressed to his throat.

"I tell him, 'One chance, bud. Tell the truth and walk away. Lie to me and you won't leave this car.'

"This tweaker was still coming up from his hit, so he just sits there trembling and staring at me." I paused in thought for a second, considering my usual appearance: stubble-whiskers, dark circles beneath bloodshot eyes, plus the way the elements have roughened my skin over nearly twenty years' worth of outside work. "Maybe I was a sight, too. The familiar kind, one troublemaker to another."

A grunt escaped the director. It might've been a laugh, since his cheeks flushed and the storm cloud of his mood grew even darker. I smirked and settled back in my chair.

"I told the tweaker, 'You made your buy in the bathroom. Is your dealer a local?'

"'He s-says so. F-from the f-f-f-forest.'

"'Was he alone?'

"'No. Th-there's another guy, but he n-n-never gets out of the truck...car...I mean—'

"'How long you been buying from him?'

"'Three m-m-months.'

"Puzzle pieces in my mind started fitting together. I'd been making bush-league meth busts here and there, mostly kids out in the woods, during the last eight weeks. Some of the park guests were talking about encountering weirdos on the remote trails. The local cops were also tracking a rise in drug abuse, and there were those mud tracks on Gordon Road. Did I have all the pieces? Nope, but I could tell what the picture looked like.

"I press the knife a little harder against the tweaker's neck. An ounce more pressure would've broken his skin, and he knew it.

"'When I'm gone,' I tell him, 'you put this car in drive and never come back. If you're local, I *strongly* suggest you call a relative or friend out of stat and go make a fresh start. If I see you again, I'll bury you so deep in the woods it'll take three hundred years and an archaeology team to find your remains, and that's only if the animals don't dig you up and drag your corpse off for lunch. Understand?'

"'Y-yes. Thank—'

"I pull back the knife at the same time I headbutt him again. This time, after his eyes cross, they roll up in his head. He sags back against the door, and I leave him there with blood dripping from his nostrils.

"The pipe and the meth go in the dumpster before I roar off in my pickup the way I'd come, and before I know it I'm parking at a picnic area a quarter mile off the trailhead where I'd noticed the tire tracks. I didn't call for backup; fifteen minutes had passed, and pretty soon the tweaker would wake up, realize he was hurt but not screwed, and make a warning call to his dealer. You know what happens when *that* happens: poof! They're gone, even if they have to ditch the lab, and the good guys are back on square one. So I pause just long enough to get my gun belt out of the lockbox in the pickup bed, strap it on, and them I'm behind the wheel and rolling.

"At that time, there was an orange rope strung between two posts where the trail enters the woods. It had a sign too: a weather-beaten thing about hunting permits and seasons and being careful because people with guns are around. I drive through the rope and hit the four-wheel drive.

"I take it slow, since I have no idea what I'll find or when I'll find it. The tire marks veer off along a fire trail. I follow and drive on for a while, and just when I'm thinking about how isolated I am, the tracks go totally off-road.

"I decide to hoof it from there. As soon as my feet hit the ground, my Colt's in my hand. I head deeper into the woods, fast but careful so I don't make much noise. After a couple minutes, the forest goes dead silent like before a storm. There's a puff of breeze, but that's it. All the bird calls and critter rustles are behind me or way off to the sides. It freaks me out, but contrary to popular thought, I actually take my job seriously, so I press on."

11

"Alone," said the director. "Against god-knows-what."

I chuckled. "You act like you don't know where this is going. Like what happened next isn't why we've got the *pleasure* of each other's company. Anyway, it's not long before I spot a trailer in a natural clearing. I can't miss the thing. It's an old, shiny-sided metal Airstream. A big camouflage net with leaves and moss and branches is stretched over it and tied to trees at the perimeter of the clearing. All the windows are blacked out with paint, and I see yellow spray-in foam on all the joints between pieces of metal, on the body of the trailer, around the windows, everywhere. Some sort of air-scrubber unit is up on the roof, ticking and humming like somebody just shut it off.

"The SUV's beneath the netting, pulled right up beside a dozen propane tanks leaning helter-skelter on the uneven ground. They're all networked into a single fat rubber rose, which feeds into the side of the Airstream. Something about the casual disorder makes me even more cautious than I've been, so I slow down and," I pursed my lips, framing what came next as I replayed events in my mind for the thousandth time, "that's when I encounter...something."

The director perked up. "Be specific."

I blew air out through my nostrils. "You know those invisible dog fences? That's what I thought of when it happened. One second I'm sneaking from tree to tree, closing in on the trailer, the next it's like I'm passing through an electrical field. It was strong but not lethal, like touching a broken bulb on a string of Christmas lights, only this was like I ran my whole body into a vertical sheet of electricity. I drop to a knee as I pass through, but like I said, I'm keyed-up so I don't think it worked as well as it was supposed to."

"How can you be sure—"

"Just shut up, okay? We're getting there. So, I drop, and I know I'm in trouble, even if I don't have a clue what's happening. I keep my eyes up and searching, so I catch the driver's door of the SUV popping open. The guy who gets out is clean-cut and totally average, not that redneck stereotype meth-cooker. He's got on jeans, worn hiking boots, and an old Donald Duck t-shirt with a hole in one sleeve. Short dark hair. Sunglasses so I can't read his eyes, but I didn't need to since he stiffens the moment he spots a ranger.

"And here's the thing: he gets out, this guy, and he looks *right* at me, no hesitation whatsoever. Whatever it was I passed through, it worked like a GPS and an alarm combined. He doesn't search, doesn't swivel his head around, he just gets out and turns to me. His hands come up packing an Uzi."

I paused, drumming my fingers on the arm of the chair, working fresh moisture into my tired mouth. My mind dwelled in the part of my past I didn't like talking about. How personal did I want to get with this fat desk jockey?

Eventually I figured, *Hell with it.* If he was giving me the boot, he'd do it knowing the exact circumstances which led me to his office. I'd also be able to get blitzed later without any regrets.

"I'm good at killing people. That's what they taught me in the Marines, and even if I couldn't care less about ninety-eight percent of the rest of the Corps' discipline and ideals, the truth is they make a fucking warrior out of you, and that never goes away. When I see that Uzi, I don't think and I sure as hell don't run. I put a .45 slug right between that bastard's eyeballs. His brains splatter pink and gray all over the shiny side of the Airstream. The guy's a corpse before his finger touches the trigger.

"A second passes where my heart's hammering and my ears are ringing. There's crimson goo dripping down the side of the Airstream. My sight's ultra-crisp thanks to an adrenalin surge, and I catch individual flutters of leaves, rays of light making spotlight-bright pools on the ground, and bugs buzzing every which way in the disturbed air. The clean parts of the Airstream are so shiny I almost miss its door flying open.

"The guy who comes out…well, I don't know what to say about him except he was *strange*. He's wearing a black robe with a hood, like something for the Renaissance Faire or Halloween. His pale face is shiny with sweat, and when he looks around for the source of the commotion, he does it like he's not used to the lay of the land. Like he's in some foreign country. Don't ask how I know that — it's a sense I get when I look at people."

"I understand," said the director.

"I doubt it," I shot back.

He smirked. "I did your job for fifteen years before I transferred to administration."

Well, *that* threw me for a loop. I didn't like doing it, but I nodded a concession and said, "I won't waste my breath, then."

"Good. This meeting is going long, and I'm due at another

soon."

I let it go. If I didn't, I was a petty asshole, and I thought of myself as a *superior* asshole. "Right. Anyway, he's got a mark on his face. I don't know if it's a tattoo or a decal or what, but one thing's damn sure, it's glowing."

I drifted back in my memory: three horizontal lines beginning at the corner of his mouth and extending most of the way toward his earlobe. Mirror the symbol on his other cheek, put a guitar in his hands, add some white pancake makeup, and he might be auditioning for a KISS cover band.

But those marks… "They're glowing blue-white, and little wisps of smoke are curling past his eyeball on that side, like the marks are burning up."

The director had his fingers tented before his face as he leaned his elbows on his desk. He showed that piss-poor poker face again, with the twitch and darting eyes, but all he said was, "Go on."

"You know something." It popped out of my mouth, but it sounded as correct as it felt.

"I know lot of things, Mister Keester."

"No, I mean you know something about that guy. You know more than I do, and now you're being a jagoff—"

"Enough!" Yehl slammed his palms on the desk, toppling his miniature American flag. His ruddy face radiated heat as he rose and leaned over the desk. When he tried planting his arms atop a stack from my file, the papers slid askew and fanned out, making him stagger like a drunk. His face turned an even darker shade of red as he swept my files onto the floor; when that was done he tried looming again. This time it worked. His tie swung like a pendulum between his rigid, trembling arms. Spittle flew from his lips when he hollered, "This is an interview, not a conversation! I ask the questions! You answer them! That's it! Do you understand?"

I pulled my gun. The end of the long barrel hovered two inches from the director's suddenly saucer-sized eyes. His breath went out in a half-grunting-sigh, and all that angry color drained from his cheeks.

"What I *understand* is that this is an exit interview, which means one way or the other I'm fucked. End of the line, so long, get out. So you'll *understand* when I say you've got jack shit for leverage."

The director, to his credit, stayed very still. "Think carefully. If you shoot me——"

"If I shoot you, it might actually make my day better." I flicked the Colt's barrel at the chair behind him. "Sit down."

To my amazement, he complied. After a second, he arched an eyebrow in a *what-now?* kind of way.

He was too calm. He probably had a panic button on the underside of his desk. I figured a platoon of Capitol Police were already locking down the building. Pretty soon, they'd be banging through the door behind me, and that would be that.

That in mind, I asked Yehl, "Do I have time for the whole story, or just the executive summary?"

He frowned, looking genuinely puzzled as nervous sweat beads rolled down his forehead. Then his eyes widened as his shoulders relaxed. "I assure you, nobody outside this room can hear or see us." He nodded at the Colt while keeping his palms flat on the desk. "Put that away. I promise not to say another word until you're finished." He sounded factual, not friendly as he slowly folded his hands, leaned back in his chair, and gave me calm, curious eyes.

His ease creeped me out. There had to be an angle here, something I was missing, but damn if I could see it.

I laid the gun along my thigh without letting go of it. "So this guy comes out with the glowing mark," I said as the details refreshed themselves in my conscious mind. "Of course, I target him and call out, 'Freeze!' and he just stands there fuming like I just raped his mother in front of him. He doesn't look at the guy from the SUV, he isn't armed, and he doesn't do a damn thing to give me an itchy trigger finger.

"I advance, slow and easy so my aim doesn't falter. The guy is muttering to himself, too soft for me to hear. I'm fifteen feet away, thinking about how it's almost over, and naturally, that's when it goes south. The marks on his cheek flare as bright as the sun. I flinch and stagger to my left, and that probably saves my life.

"The guy throws out his arms. Something shoots out from between his hands, right at me. It's..." I sighed, then chuckled. "Ah, shit, this sounds dumb as hell, but it's like a blob of shadow. It's black and about the size of my fist, and jiggling like a water balloon. It zips past my head, missing by an inch or two, and making a noise like somebody wiggling sheet metal: *blo-oob! blo-oob! blo-oob!* Then it hits a tree behind me.

"I shit you not, the spot it hits disintegrates. I'm finding my balance and getting set for a shot, and then there's this sound behind me of wood splintering. *Big* wood. It comes again, loud and popping, and I look over my shoulder.

"Three quarters of the foot-wide maple's trunk is gone from head to waist height. It's like somebody came in there with a giant ice cream scoop. The black blob is evaporating in gray wisps of smoke as it dissolves the trunk, but I only get a quick look since the rest of the tree is falling straight at my face.

"I throw myself sideways. The tree misses, but it makes this crashing boom that's half-heard, half-felt from so close a range. I roll into a crouch facing the man just as he throws out another blob. I roll again. This time, I stay down, flat in the dirt with my gun pointing at him. I shoot until my revolver clicks empty. I peg him again and again, center mass. He shakes with the impacts, but that's it. He's staring at me like nothing's wrong as I run out of bullets and keep dry-pulling the trigger. Just standing there with a shirt full of holes, with the marks still flaring, and an asshole-smile on his lips. He's up there on the trailer's little porch, looking down at me like he's a king and I was the only one of his subjects who actually went through with the uprising.

"So I'm out of ammo…but not weapons. I drop the Colt, get my right foot beneath me, and rise to a knee. As I push the rest of the way up, I draw my knife from my boot. It's one of those all-metal jobs, balanced for throwing. The guy doesn't see it until it's flying out of my hand, and the next thing either of us knows, the blade's buried in his chest. No bullshit, watching that guy double over was one of the best feelings I've had in a long time."

I paused, thinking back, reliving what came next. "Either he should've screamed or just dropped dead. Instead, he straightens up and *smiles* at me. His teeth are brown and they're *all* pointy, like a mouthful of rotten fangs. There's no splash of blood, no look of pain on his face, and just like that I'm in a slasher flick where the bad guy keeps coming and coming no matter what you do to him. He yanks the knife out and then tosses it behind him, into the trailer."

I hesitated before telling the director the details I'd left out of my official statements. "My heart starts racing so fast I can't think. The guy's cheek blazes again. This time the marks *move*, man, down his cheek and his neck, to his right arm, all the way to his the first three fingers on that hand. When he flings out that hand, three black blobs erupt, all at the same time.

"I hit the deck and roll around in the half-assed cover of the fallen tree's limbs. Those sheet metal noises chase me, and then I'm crouching, leaping, falling, scrambling as I realize that this time those blobs aren't evaporating on impact. I finally roll beside the SUV's passenger door so the truck is between me and the weirdo, and I get about two seconds to catch my breath before the three blobs start circling overhead like a swarm of RC helicopters. One floats down in front me, then stops while the other two spread out to the sides.

"I know a flanking move when I see it, and I know it means I'm in deep shit, so I force my eyes to move, seek, look for an out.

"'Enough of this!' the guy calls out. 'Surrender or die.'

"To my left is the network of propane tanks. I kept searching, knowing that even if I had my Colt or the dead guy's Uzi, you can't really blow those suckers up like they do in the movies…but then I hear the blobs' noises around me and think about that tree trunk getting gouged to almost nothing. How that has to take a hell of a lot of energy.

"I trust my gut and climb to my feet, then slide over by the SUV's hood so I can see the guy, and pop up my middle finger. 'Up yours!' I yell as I run for the propane tanks. 'No surrender!'

"The guy hisses and says, 'Then you die!'

"The blobs make their noises around me. I hear them cutting through the air right behind me and sprint as fast I can. When I get to the tanks I jump and stretch myself out, flying through the air head-first as I clear the equipment and slide in the loose earth and grass. It hurts like a bitch, but there's no time for pain. I get my knees under me, then my feet, and push off to the right in a dead run.

"The blobs go low when I go low, which I was counting on. They impact the tanks…or maybe disintegrate them is a better term. I don't know for sure because looking back isn't on my radar, but *something* crazy happened. I hear three sounds like *thung-thung-thung!* and then a *whump!*. There's a flash of white fire, and I don't see much else because I'm too busy diving into a shallow ravine just inside the treeline making myself small against what's surely coming next. There's not much of a wait. The boom when it all goes up ruffles my hair and clothes and sends a fireball over my head.

"The guy in black screams, but not so loud as the trailer's metal sides tearing apart like lunchmeat. I want to look, the same way people want to look at train wrecks, but I'm not stupid. I stay prone until half a propane tank stabs a jagged knife of metal in the ground less than a yard from my face. That's when I decide distance is a better bet than cover, so I get my feet under me and take a look around.

"Even before that day, I knew I was lucky not to have been involved with a big forest fire. I've seen them on TV, talked to guys who've fought them, but nothing prepares you for the sight of it. The meth lab's a fan of curled and blackened metal. Piss-colored smoke billows out. Ahead of that is a crater where the propane tanks once stood. The SUV's got a big wedge of steel through its windshield, and the paint on the whole front end is peeled back like a camouflage potato skin.

"Beyond the blast damage, there's nothing but fire. It's climbing the trees, eating up all that drought-dry timber. The heat's pushing at me like an open oven, and even though watching the flames dance has a certain hypnotic quality to it, I know I need to get the hell out of there. I pick my way over to my Colt, snatch it up, and run for my life."

The director leaned forward. "That fire destroyed a fifth of the park before it was contained."

My eyes narrowed as my blood pressure shot up. Each heartbeat thrummed in my ears. "Yeah. I know. I oversaw the containment effort."

"From your office on the other side of the park."

"Yep."

"Where you keep you liquor."

"Hey: fuck you. I wasn't drinking."

"Says the man who *was* drinking before all of this happened."

I stood up and pointed a finger at Yehl's chest. "Enough. Yeah, I drink. A little on the job, a lot after. I'm divorced. I'm wage-garnished for alimony the ex doesn't need. I don't even have a place to *put* a pot to piss in. I don't like anybody but my dog, and I suppose you could say I'm a step away from just tuning out and never giving a shit again. Okay? That's the truth, and here's some more: I burned down a fifth of the forest doing my job. I took the mandate and enforced it. I stopped the manufacture and distribution of illegal drugs on state land, and I did it without shedding any innocent blood.

Maybe you can't agree with my methods publicly, but deep down I think you do, since nobody's had me arrested." I holstered my weapon as Yehl's eyes went from fear to shock to confusion like flipping through a picture book where every page illustrates a different emotion.

I yanked my ID off its clip on my chest pocket and flung it onto the desk. "You want my head over a forest fire, fine. I guess I shouldn't expect any more from an ass-kisser at a desk, even if you really did do my job like you said." I laughed without a touch of mirth. "The truth is, you need guys like me, both to do the dirty stuff *and* to take the fall. *That's* bureaucracy, right?" I sat back down, feeling lighter for venting all that steam.

The director wore one of his red-faced frowns. He held himself tense but still as he asked. "Do you need to add anything further?"

"No—yes. The guy in the black robe. I didn't see any blood or body parts on my way out, not even a scrap of fabric. It makes me sad."

Yehl's eyes narrowed. "Sad?"

"That I'm not sure the son of a bitch is dead. Anybody who takes a pass at me and gets away with it is a bad day waiting to happen, somewhere down the line." I drummed my fingers on the edge of the desk. "Man, I wish I knew for sure if I got him!"

"You did," a man's voice spoke up behind me.

I reacted without thought. I planted my boot soles flush on the front of Yehl's desk and pushed. Chair legs shrieked over hardwood until I rammed whoever it was behind me. He grunted and doubled over on impact. I caught a peripheral glimpse of a black hood spilling around a pale face, and then I was rising, drawing the Colt, swinging the long barrel in an uppercut whip.

Whatever tricks he'd pulled in the woods didn't save him from taking iron upside the head. He grunted and went down in a limp heap. I followed, thumbing back the Colt's hammer as I straddled his narrow frame and rammed the barrel into his gasping mouth.

My whole body tingled with rage, vengeance, and adrenalin-fueled surprise. The cold satisfaction I always felt when I got a second chance at somebody who'd bested me was like jet fuel dumped on a bonfire.

"Well, well," I said as he tasted gun oil and grew very still. My free left hand reached up and tapped his unmarked cheek. "I'm guessing from the look in your eyes that your skills aren't worth shit unless you're wearing that light-up tattoo." I eased the gun a little deeper down his throat, and he gagged around it. "I'm also guessing you wish you hadn't fucked with me, but it's way too late for apologies and buying me a round. So, asshole, let's just say, 'So long.' Okay?" I put pressure on the trigger—

"Stop!" yelled the director.

My finger eased back, but I did not take my eyes off the dude beneath me. My whole body vibrated with potential, almost like I'd stopped having sex just before the big finish.

"Why?" I asked. My voice trembled.

"You'll ruin an original nineteenth-century floor."

I twitched through the shoulders as my mind went over a cliff. It made me look at my Yehl despite myself. "That's the last thing I expected."

The director held up both hands. He looked almost as pale as the guy beneath me, but his was the pallor of horror. "I had to get your attention."

"I don't need to see him to shoot him."

"That would be a mistake."

I sneered. "I don't give a shit about your vintage floor, and I don't have much left to lose here."

"Wrong."

"Oh, please."

"I'm serious, Mister Keester. You aren't being fired." He pointed a finger at the man beneath me without lowering his arm. "At least, I don't think so."

I looked down at the guy in black, at his growing serenity despite his predicament. "Okay, I'm lost."

"Take the gun out of his mouth. Please?"

I hesitated, but didn't change my gaze as I spoke to both of them. "If there's a *tic* of movement I don't like, both of you die. Simple as that."

"You'll go to jail," said Yehl.

"Ask me if I give a shit."

"I think you do. You're might be a killer, but you're no murderer."

Damn, he had me there. I yanked the Colt out as I rocked back into a crouch, then got up and turned sideways to put my back to the fireplace. I took a two-handed grip and pointed the barrel at the antique floor.

"Talk," I said as my eyes flicked back and forth between them.

The guy in black sat up without using his hands, like a cheesy vampire popping out of a coffin. When he smiled, I got another look at his mouthful of brown fangs. He climbed to his feet slowly, studying me with crawling eyes like I was a lot up for auction. "He will suit."

"Pardon?" I said.

The director cleared his throat. "Ranger, this is Shadowheart, Lord Ruler of the High Coven of Warlocks in the Enchanted Forest State Forest."

My mouth popped open, but once it did I couldn't frame a response. I wound up sneering at Yehl with my left eyebrow arching as high as it would go.

"You remember the big news from last spring, don't you?"

I put two and two together. "The Enchanted Forest thing? That wasn't a joke?"

Yehl looked taken aback. "Why would you think that?"

"You made the announcement on April Fool's Day."

"Oh, who thinks about things like that?"

"Everybody not in the government, from all the PR I've been doing."

Yehl's mouth opened, but like me, he couldn't immediately find words to match his perplexed expression. He rubbed a finger through his mustache until he got a hold of himself. "The timing doesn't matter. The point is, the Enchanted Forest has been annexed by the state, and Lord Shadowheart here is a representative of that place."

I put my attention back on the…warlock. He didn't even have the decency to quit staring when I focused on him, which meant I went on feeling like a fillet in a meat case. "Let's get to the part where you explain how you're standing here, yet still claiming I blew you up with the meth lab."

"Let's all sit down," Yehl said

"No, we're fine as we are." I caught the warlock's eyes. "Start talking."

His eyes flashed with the haughty defiance of the privileged, and he drew himself more fully erect. It made me think, *you could switch him and Yehl, just change who does what. They're the same type.*

Shadowheart loosed an overwrought sigh. "Much of what a warlock does is secret. We are a small order, and—"

"I don't need backstory," I told him.

"You need some," he shot back. "You need to know that…" His mouth twisted like he'd just found a nugget of shit under his tongue. "There are only five of us, though we appear to be many more. You see, we can split our minds into many functional vessels, which we call aspects."

I cocked my head, looking for the lie on his face and finding the opposite. A glance at Yehl yielded a shrug.

"Oh-kaaaay…" I prompted.

"When the people of the Enchanted Forest exposed ourselves to the human world, we knew there were risks of contamination," said Shadowheart.

Yehl added. "He's talking about drugs, Ranger. They knew about them, but they had no idea how fast they'd become an issue."

I nodded. "Nobody does, until it's already happening."

Shadowheart's jaw jutted out as his eyes drew back into memory. "When it became apparent that my lands were becoming a favorite spot for meth cookers, I sent an aspect of myself to hunt down the lab."

More connecting of dots, bam-bam-bam. "Your aspect went rogue, didn't he?"

The warlock twitched before he could stop himself. He looked like he was reevaluating his opinion of me. "That's right."

A grim smile framed my extrapolations. "He found the lab, got hooked on meth, then got convinced by the guy I shot that he could be a bigshot distributor out in the real world…my world…you know what I mean." Another connection: "And when the cooker found out this aspect could do…" I arched an eyebrow. "Magic?" A nod. "Okay, *magic* out here, so long as he had that glowing mark on his cheek, it was just a matter of time."

Yehl said, "You've gone to the core of it—"

Still looking at Shadowheart, I said, "Just a matter of time until you end up screwing up my forest and my job, maybe my whole life. Right, shithead?"

He bristled. "It wasn't me. It was an aspect—"

"Oh, don't split hairs. The aspect is a part of you, isn't it?"

"An aspect has freedom of will and thought."

"So you're gonna stand there and tell me you created something from thin air or whatever, over which you have no control, or thrall, or whatever fancy term you want to use? That you just popped it in, sent it out, and made it promise to run its errand and get home before the streetlights came on?"

"How dare you take that tone with me!"

I rolled my eyes. "Don't give me that high-and-mighty crap. You're here because you're in as much trouble as me for letting that aspect thing maraud around." I looked at Yehl. "Right?"

A smile crossed the director's lips.

The warlock kept sputtering. "I will not be spoken to in this way! I have protected and nurtured my lands for—"

"Blah-blah-blah," I cut in. "That's the past. The *now* is that you blew it by not keeping tabs on your aspect. You caused a disaster, and that's all there is to it."

"Do not insult me, human."

"First of all, I think I already did. Second, how are you gonna stop me without a mark on your face?"

His eyes hardened. "Shall I show you?"

I brought the Colt to bear on him, center-mass. "Whenever you're ready, tough guy."

The director clapped his hands. "Enough!" His mustache bristled like a living, angry creature. "This pissing contest isn't constructive. You *both* made serious errors. You're *both* much too cocky for you own good. Lord Shadowheart, the Ranger is correct in what he says. Any method you devise for dealing with a problem is your responsibility. Given that this situation occurred outside of your normal lands and experiences, you should've shown more initiative towards oversight. Do you agree?"

The warlock grunted.

"You approve of him? Do I have you binding word on behalf of the Queen?"

"We have no queen, but I'm sure you mean the princess—"

"Whatever. Do I have your word?"

Shadowheart gave me another once-over. "You do."

"Good. You're dismissed. Go back to your people and spread the word about him before he arrives. It'll be better if everybody's prepared."

"Wait, wait," I said. "What word?"

The director held up a finger as he locked eyes with Shadowheart, who broke contact first and said, "As you command."

"We call them orders here," said the director. "You'll receive more."

The warlock almost retorted, thought better of it, and offered a curt nod. He turned to me in a billow of black cloak. His eyes fell to my Colt, and even though I didn't want to, I holstered it. The gun was only part of my mojo, after all.

"We will meet again, I'm sure." He started past me.

I caught his arm. He bared his pointy teeth. Up close they looked even more freakish and disgusting. A trickle of fear slid down my spine like icy water, but I kept my eyes flinty and my voice harsh.

"If we do, keep your goddamn aspects to yourself. Got it?"

"You—" Shadowheart hissed as I squeezed a pressure point near his elbow.

"I'm not interested in your opinion. Tell me you understand and we can both get on with our lives."

Seconds passed, long enough for me to wonder if I'd made a mistake, but the warlock finally said, "I understand."

I let go. Shadowheart shook his arm as he scowled at me. "So *you* understand, Ranger," he said in one of those soft-yet-creepy voices favored by psychos, "I am never powerless."

Fast as a blink, the warlock vanished. In his place was a shimmering patch of air, like a human-shaped heat haze. It moved past me. Yehl's office door swung open and stayed that way, squeaking on a neglected hinge. The secretary gaped at the mostly-invisible warlock as he passed her desk, then remembered her job and, rising, closed the door.

I looked at the director. "Okay, enough crypticism. What exactly am I acceptable for?"

The director resettled himself in his cushy leather office chair and started reorganizing the remains of his bureaucratic paperwork stacks. From the way his face contorted as he did it, he was wrestling with something in his mind. Eventually he said, "I'm promoting you."

My head reeled. "That wasn't what I was expecting."

The director's smile turned cunning as he looked up at me. "The Enchanted Forest has been a part of Illinois for months now. It's no

joke, and it's filled with creatures we don't understand in the least."
He finished his sorting and interlaced his fingers. "Nobody has any
idea what to do with the place. That's where you come in."

I was connecting dots again, but the picture they revealed only
made the most rudimentary sense. My mouth worked, but again I
couldn't put together enough sounds for words.

Yehl's smile grew. Dammit, he was enjoying watching me
squirm. "The Enchanted Forest is now under my purview. In fact,
I'm taking on a new role in addition to my current responsibilities.
You, Mister Keester, are looking at the first-ever director of the Illinois Department of Unnatural Resources."

I snorted. "DUR? You'd pronounce that as, 'dur?'"

"That's right."

"That's the sound I make when I think of morons."

"Well, you might want to reevaluate, since you've been transferred to DUR."

My sneer fell apart. "Pardon me?"

"You are now *Sheriff* Keester of the Enchanted Forest State Forest, with full police powers and an authority level equal to any other
Officer in Charge. You'll enforce the law, liaise with the rest of the
state and local government, including those authorities present within the Forest—"

"Wait, wait." I put my hands on my hips. "You're serious about
this, aren't you?"

"Very serious."

"I start a forest fire, shoot a drug dealer, drink on the job, then
threaten you in your own office, and you're *promoting* me?" A nasty
cackle erupted from my throat. "It really is true. The government
takes care of the fuckups better than the honest folks."

Yehl's face turned red again. His nostrils flared as he took a series
of measured breaths. When he spoke, his words came hard, clipped,
and mean. "You're right. I *am* promoting a fuckup. One who burned
down more timber than anybody else in Illinois, ever. A man who
shits on the rules whenever it suits him, then claims no fault when
the inevitable trouble finds him. A man ruined by liquor and the lais-
sez-faire attitude of highway repair crews and postal workers.

"You want to know why I'm doing it? Why you're getting broad
authority and power? Quite simply, you're the governor's wife's ex-
husband, and they feel sorry for you. That's right. They know even

better than me what a waste of life you are, and while they can't quite bring themselves to cut you loose, they *can* take this rather unique opportunity to both get you out of the way and put your contrary surliness to good use."

His derision cut me, but I took that pain and channeled it into nastiness. Hearing the hard parts of my life recited like a grocery list pressed all my rage buttons at once. "Pass. I quit. Fuck this and fuck you."

Yehl flashed his real smile, the one behind the bureaucrat that let me see his triumph. I knew I was screwed before he spoke. "Quit, and you go up on destruction of state property, manslaughter, and attempted murder charges, plus you'll lose your job for gross misconduct. You'll spend the better part of whatever time an asshole like you has left in a supermax prison with all the really bad apples, and I'll make sure I have a permanent CC feed of you so I can see just how long it takes them to break you."

We stared at one another while I ran odds on escaping the building if I shot him. Yehl watched me do it, all the while keeping that smile on his face like a dare. Like he knew exactly how tight a corner he'd put me in. "This is blackmail."

The director nodded. "Of course it is." He reached into his desk and pulled out a large envelope bearing a state seal I'd never before encountered:

He passed it to me. I felt paper and a hunk of metal inside. Probably a badge, but if it wasn't, I'd requisition one on the state's dime. Every lawman needs a badge.

"This is a clean slate for you, Sheriff," the director said. I expect you to make something of that place, not just sit on your ass and be the schmoe you've been for years." His doubtful face told me what he thought of my chances. "Until I know you're taking things seriously, the investigation into the fire will remain open."

Figures, I thought as I looked from him to the envelope to mess of mingled paperwork scattered across the desk and floor. I had zero doubts he could turn all that information against me.

I eyeballed my boss as I laid down the envelope. "Clean slate, huh?"

"That's right."

I held out my right hand. "Have I got your word on it?"

He hesitated, then got up and came around the desk to clasp my hand. "My word. A clean slate."

"Excellent." I swung my left fist in a hook, catching him on the jaw and twisting him around. He splattered against his big windows and squeaked his way down, inch by inch, out cold.

"That'll get wiped off my record, right?" I asked as I picked up the envelope. I left the office and took the stairs down to a ground-level fire exit. Out I went, even though it set off alarms which would likely force everybody outside into the midday oven of downstate Illinois in the grips of a late-summer drought. I headed straight for my pickup and drove away without a look back. I was a troublemaker, but only a *dumbass* troublemaker hangs around to watch the aftermath when he can Google it later.

I was fifty miles down the highway before my government-issued cell phone rang. I sent the call to voicemail, then chuckled as the caller tried a second time. At that point, I rolled down my window and tossed the phone onto the rolling asphalt. It shattered in a spray of black plastic debris in my rear-view mirror, and then I was over a hill and gone and my fingers were on the radio. Guns N' Roses blared sleazy anger: "Out Ta Get Me." I cranked it up and screeched along with Axl while I dwelled for some damn reason on destiny. The thing was, I always envisioned destiny as a happy achievement or a place to call home. Instead, it was just the frayed end of my twisted professional line. There wasn't another chance, another place, another do-over around the bend if I messed this up. Hell, there wasn't even another bend to go around. Just a brick wall stretching out as far as I could see, with only a narrow tunnel for my life's road. I could fit, but I sensed there wasn't room for detour or distraction.

Most people would find that scary. For me, it was liberating. One chance, one way, no mulligans. It sounded like focus.

Okay, I told myself. *The Enchanted Forest State Forest. I'll do it up right.*

A while later, I took the exit leading to the state-owned house I'd lived in since transferring to my now-former park. I'd collect my dog, my liquor, and whatever else I needed, then hit the road before Yehl sent somebody after me. Let him worry for a little bit, then show up at this new place down south on my own terms. Nobody realized it yet, but a clean slate meant I got to break some rules all over again, since I had no reprimands in my file.

The Enchanted Forest State Forest, I thought again. *Even the name is weird, but that's okay. So am I.*

August 10, 2013
October 6, 2017

Marie Otte

Marie Otte is an astrologer, meditation teacher and member of the Fox Valley Writers Group. She has had short stories and poems published in three of the Batavia Library Writers Workshop Annuals. "Commanding Influences" and "Poetic Music Makers" are two poetry books that she self-published. Marie has had magazine articles published in Quest, Sat Vidhya Ezine and Dreamnetwork.net. Currently, she is writing a book about spirituality.

Can You?

Can you get along without
Food, water, shelter, clothing?

Can you get along without
Computers, phones, devices?

Can you get along without
Fashion show designer clothes?

Can you get along without
Chateaus, villas, grand mansions?

Can you get along without
Exorbitant jewelry?

Can you get along without
Limousines, sports cars, air planes?

Can you get along without
Luxury yachts, real fast jets?

Can you get along without
True friends, love of family?

You can decide what you can get along without
Prioritize!

Extra Money

"Wait a minute. That's not right!" Angel said as he read his bank balance statement in disbelief.

"Go ahead and enjoy it!"

"Hold on. Where did this extra deposit come from? I am going to close my eyes and this $10,000 will be gone from my statement."

"It's still there, huh? Come on, open your eyes."

Jim opened his eyes and said, "$10,000 in my account? I don't know where that came from. I have to call the bank and let them know that there has been some kind of mistake."

"Hold on my friend. This is a wonderful opportunity. Go ahead and enjoy it. You know, this happens to others."

"It's not mine. It's not right! I'm going to notify the bank."

"Don't do it. How many honest people do you actually know?"

"I know plenty!"

"Who? Name one."

Angel started to perspire and could feel his heart pumping faster. He stalled coming up with a name by taking several sips of water from his glass. Angel was silent because he couldn't come up with one.

"Maybe your dad or brother?"

"Don't go bringing them up. They got a bum rap."

"Just face it, they got caught stealing money. The store taped them on a surveillance camera taking money out of the cash register. You are the only honest person I know. That is why you deserve this extra money. No one will know."

"I will know. It's not honest"

"You deserve some new clothes. Get yourself a suit, cuff links and a tie tack. Maybe some new jeans and shirts for that casual designer look."

"I could use some new threads. Maybe just a few things."

"Remember all of those projects you put on hold? Paint the inside of your house. Spruce up the place. Get some new furniture."

"Yeah! Yeah!!! That shouldn't cost too much."

"What about Crystal?"

"Crystal? Don't go bringing her into this."

"Yeah, Crystal from work. You are crazy about her."

"Wait a minute. How do you know how I feel about her?"

"I know everything. Ask her out on a date. I bet she'll go."

"Go out with me?"

"Take her out to an Italian restaurant for some calamari, lasagna and tira-misu. Go and see a nice play. That would impress her."

"That would be kind of nice. I was just thinking about Chicken Marsala and Broadway musicals."

"Every woman likes flowers. Get her a dozen red roses. Red is for love."

"Okay, but that's it."

"What about your train set in the basement? You stopped working on it a couple of years ago because of your budget. You can get that 2-4-4 locomotive ready to go and be able to buy some miniature landscaping to go around the tracks to impress your buddies. You always complained about not having money. Just do it! I'm behind you. Angel, your secret is safe with me."

"Thanks, Devil."

Wedding Review

"What a day!" he said as he walked out of the bathroom.

"It couldn't have been better," she said as she kicked off her slippers and laid down on the bed.

"Why did that little girl cry going down the aisle?"

"Shy, I guess. There were a lot of people in the church. Oh well, she started smiling halfway through the ceremony."

"Flower girls should be at least 13 years old. Don't cha think?"

"At that age, she wouldn't be a flower girl anymore. She would be a junior bridesmaid."

"I've never heard of that. I didn't realize that weddings were so complicated."

"I know, that's why Lisa and I planned everything, as long as you footed the bill."

"I've been doing that for years."

"And you're very good at it," she winked her eye at him.

"Once that kid dropped the rings, I thought they were gone for good."

"I guess they didn't have the ribbons tied tight enough on the rings. That's why they fell off the ring bearer's pillow. The minister has good eyesight. He found both of them right away over by the baptismal font."

"The soloist could have used some more voice lessons. Her High C's fell flat."

"Oh, that was your cousin. Have a heart."

"It took forever for Lisa and Craig to light that big candle."

"Oh well, that means they will be together forever."

"It was so great when Lisa threw the bouquet into the chandelier by accident. Your aunt Mary fought to get it down. SPLASH! Right into the punch bowl. Your Aunt must be determined to marry her fourth husband. Wait a minute, is her last divorce final, yet?"

"Today brought back memories. When Lisa was little, do you remember when you dressed her up to be a bride?"

"Oh, yeah! She would not tell me why she wanted to be a bride that year," she said while she fluffed up her pillow.

"When we picked her up from that Halloween party, she had fake blood all over her costume. Jimmy Meyers wore a great count outfit. He was Dracula and she became his bride. They had it planned ahead of time. He brought a tube of red stuff to the party. What a trickster. You should have seen the look on your face."

"I was so startled to see that red stuff all over her. I thought she got hurt. She knew I would never let her do that. Ya know, now that I think about it, it was kinda cute. I am looking forward to becoming a grandma!"

"Wait a minute … is Lisa pregnant?"

"No, I'm just so excited from today. Just thinking ahead."

"I hope they wait a bit. Probably not. They have been living in sin for two years."

"Who cares?"

"If they have a baby, does that mean I'm gonna have to pay for another shower and a baptismal party? Does that involve another expensive wedding planner?"

"No, I can do those on my own. I'm so glad they are going to Hawaii for their honeymoon. That's where we went, remember? It was so romantic."

"The islands, flowers and food were so good. We should do it again. Maybe do a cruise this time so we don't have to walk so much. Maybe we can have our own little honeymoon right now."

He didn't hear her respond so he rolled over to face her side of the bed. His bride of thirty years had her eyes shut and started to snore. He smiled, kissed her gently on the cheek and covered her up with the blanket.

Ric Waters

Ric Waters has dabbled in a variety of genres during his writing career, from newswriting to science fiction, suspense and historical fiction. In addition to having his stories in four previous Fox Valley Writers Group book projects, his work has appeared in "Familiar Spirits," an anthology of horror stories published by Donald J. Bingle. He self-published his first book, "History's Left Turn," an anthology of thirty alternate-history flash-fiction stories, in March 2017. Also, he published 14 fan-fiction stories based on the cult-classic science-fiction series "SLIDERS" (alternateslides.wordpress.com) and four novellas based on the "Doctor Who" parody "Inspector Spacetime" (btvbooks.wordpress.com/titles). Ric resides in Aurora, Illinois.

Fleeing from the Dark

The night air had turned crisp, but the clear skies made for a beautiful night to put on a fire and enjoy the peace.

I had cut some wood earlier in the day and set it along the back wall of the cabin I had rented for the week. It had been a bargain, since the camping season had only begun that week and the long winter seemed to have kept many people home. The days had turned reasonably nice, not quite warm, but pleasant enough. The forest preserve offered plenty of trails to hike for exercise and the opportunity to view local wildlife.

After retrieving some split logs from the pile, I stacked them two across, then two more perpendicularly, then two more layers before stuffing some newspaper between the wood and finally lighting it. As the logs started to catch fire, I brought out a plastic lawn chair from inside the cabin to sit on.

A few crickets chirped in the darkness around me, but it wasn't warm enough for them to be seeking each others' company. The almost-full moon hung in the sky, creating a jagged, black silhouette of the forest that surrounded the cabin. A few stray clouds scudded across the sky, muting the moonlight as they passed between the moon and Earth.

The fire snapped and crackled as it bit into the wood and fed on it. Flames danced happily along the logs and in the spaces between them. I decided to toss another log on top of the fire as it grew, figuring that I might have a few hours to enjoy the night.

A coyote howled off in the far distance. A moment later, another howl answered from another direction. Nothing to worry about, I reminded myself. Coyotes didn't get this close to the cabins. At least, that's what the park ranger had said when I checked in.

"Howl all you will," I muttered to the coyotes. "I'm not going anywhere."

I grabbed a small branch that lay on the ground and poked at the firewood, shifting the logs and causing them to spit sparks and making the flames dance again.

I was about to drop the stick and settle down in my chair when I heard the first rustlings a short distance away. Not sure what I was facing, I held the stick up like a sword, as if I could fight off something with such a flimsy weapon. I took the first few steps around the back of the cabin and tried to look into the dark woods for some sign of what was coming towards me.

The distant rustling became crashes and whip-cracks as whatever it was closed in on me. The moonlight pooled a short way from where the woods opened up next to the cabin. The noises kept getting closer and I tightened up my muscles, getting ready to fight whatever came out of the woods.

Seconds passed before I noticed movement, but before I could think what it was, it came barreling out of the darkness and collided with me, knocking me right to the ground.

I heard labored breathing, followed by the sound of something moving. I turned over to see a young woman struggling to get to her feet, while breathing so hard that it must have hurt.

I managed to get to my feet before she could get up.

"It's okay," I said quickly.

She turned to look at me. Her face was a mess of sweat, matted hair and fresh blood. She'd suffered a cut on her forehead and one below her left eye and looked terrified. She tried to catch her breath as she sat there in a crouch, ready to spring back into action to get away.

"I'm not going to hurt you," I offered gently.

Her head whipped around behind me and there was a crashing sound.

"Can't —" she blurted breathlessly.

She managed to stand up and looked about to take off running again, but she was still breathing hard and gulping air as quickly as she could.

Branches snapped and something huge loomed at the edge of the forest. It appeared to have come to a stop and roared fiercely in our direction. I turned to see her take off. I dashed after her and grabbed her wrist.

"The cabin!" I called.

She tried to shake off my hand, but I held her tightly, slowing her down. She reduced her gait to a jog, but only to slap at my hand on her. "Let ... me ... go!"

"No!" I shouted.

The beast bellowed from its hiding place in the dark woods.

"Get ... get to the cabin!" I blurted, trying to keep up with her.

By that point, the beast had abandoned the safety of the darkness, ignoring the fire and loping after us.

"Let go!" she howled at me.

I was losing my grip on her and she was clearly trying to run faster. We were quickly approaching the other edge of the clearing, then plunged headlong into the tree branches. I just let myself be dragged along behind her after she gave up trying to shake me off. Now, I was running for my life as much as she was hers. Branches and twigs flew at me from all sides, whipping my head and face. I felt something sting my right ear, followed shortly afterwards by a warm ooze. I didn't have time to think about it, I just ran along with the woman.

Not having run all that much lately, I found myself gasping for air as we fled from the beast that was gaining on us. It was difficult to think about anything, but somewhere in my oxygen-deprived brain, the thought came to the fore: Climb a tree!

"A tree!" I blurted between breaths. "We have ... to ... climb a tree!"

She jerked her hand free of my grip that had gotten loose as sweat had filled my palm. "What?!" She didn't slow down.

"Climb a ... tree!" I huffed.

"Why?"

"Bears ... bears can't ... climb trees!"

Despite the fact that she was clearly focused on escaping from the monster behind us, the statement got through to her.

"Climb a tree!" she blurted.

Before I knew it, she came to a stop and looking up at the tree trunks around us. She said nothing, simply jumped up to grab a thick branch above her and pulled herself up. The beast clumped up behind me, so I was right behind her.

We climbed up at least seven feet before finding branches to sit on while we caught our breaths. Beneath us, the black beast stopped, clearly sensing that our paths had disappeared. There was rustling around the trunk as it circled the tree. In the darkness of the forest, it was difficult to see much more than a shaggy outline.

The two of us clung to opposite sides of the trunk on facing branches, gulping air while trying to stay as quiet as we could. The creature circled the base of the trunk a couple more times before growling angrily. It seemed to fold in on itself somewhat, but what it was really doing was getting onto its hind feet and then crashed against the tree.

"Fuck!" the woman blurted.

Scared that the beast below might knock us off, I tried to cling harder to the tree. It bounced against the trunk a few more times, but it wasn't enough to jostle us loose. The creature gave up its attempt to get us out of the tree, circled around the trunk a few more times, then with a mournful wail, it lumbered off into the darkness.

We waited there for nearly an hour, concerned that the beast might return for another go at it, but there were no signs it was coming back. I had to coax the young woman out of the tree. Despite the fact that we'd both been threatened by the creature at the same time, it was clear she still didn't trust me.

Once we'd gotten back to the clearing near my cabin, I reached up to touch her face, but she pulled back and took a swing at me.

"Look," I said sternly, "you need to get those cuts treated or you'll have major problems."

The fear was still in her eyes, but she relaxed a bit. "Sorry, it hasn't been a good night."

I led her into the cabin and had her sit at the kitchen table, while I went to boil some water to clean her up. I grabbed hand towels from the linen closet, not concerned that they'd be tough to clean if any blood got on them. From the medicine cabinet, I picked up Bactine to clean and sterilize the wounds.

She slumped in the chair and looked around the main room of the cabin. "Nice place."

I offered her a smile. "It's a rental. I'm just here for the week. Vacation. Relaxation."

"Must be nice."

"It has been," I admitted.

I put a bowl in front of her and poured some hot water into it. She didn't wait for me, picked up a towel and put it into the water. She wrung it out a bit and cringed at the heat as she rubbed her face with it.

"Careful!" I warned her.

I took the towel from her hand as soon as she pulled it from her face, which came away reddened by the sudden heat bringing her capalaries to the surface. I dipped it in the hot water again, wrung it out, then dipped it again. With a practiced hand, I dabbed the cuts on her face.

"You're pretty good at this," she said as I returned the towel to the bowl.

I gave a quick laugh. "I've done this a few times before. When you spend time outdoors, you learn how to treat cuts, bites, bruises: Carefully."

She finally broke into a smile. "Thank you."

"You're welcome," I replied, returning to cleaning her wounds. "What were you doing out there, anyhow?"

She closed her eyes, since she couldn't look away. "Running."

"Yeah, I noticed that. Why?"

"To get away."

"From that bear or whatever?"

"Uh, yeah."

I wasn't convinced, but let it go. "I have Bactine to cleanse the wounds." I waited for her to respond. "Or, I think I might have iodine. Your choice."

"I don't care," she finally said.

I spritzed some Bactine onto another clean towel and carefully applied it. She cringed and hissed as the antibacterial liquid entered the wounds, but she didn't say anything. The bandages were still in the bathroom, so I had to go get them.

When I returned, she had moved to the couch. I handed the box of Band-Aids to her. "Might help keep the wounds clean."

She accepted the box, opened it and pulled out a couple of bandages. She touched the cuts tenderly before placing the strips across them.

"I don't mean to pry," I began.

"Then don't."

Okay, I thought. Not going to get answers this way. "Fine, I won't. You can stay the night, but I'd like some explanation in the morning."

She looked at me, shrugged and said, "Sure."

"Would you at least tell me your name? I'm Ted."

She shifted in her seat. "Cassandra. People call me Cassie."

"Well, nice to meet you, Cassie."

"I'd say likewise, but considering the circumstances ..."

I didn't argue the point. "There's an extra bathrobe in the bathroom, if you'd like to shower."

"Not right now," Cassandra replied. "I think I'll just crash."

I showered, making sure to lock the bathroom door, so I didn't get a surprise. She was laid out on the sofa. I went to check and she was asleep, breathing shallowly. I took that as a signal and went to bed.

When I woke the next morning, I found her clothing in a pile on the bathroom floor and water dripping from the shower head but she didn't appear to be around. I found a note on the kitchen table:

"Thanks for fixing me up last night. Sorry for all the trouble. — Cass"

I carried the note outside and looked around, called her name, but there was no one there to answer. Almost as soon as I realized that, I noticed that my pickup truck wasn't where I'd parked it. I ran inside the cabin to check my dresser and discovered that the keys were missing. One of the drawers was also just ajar. She'd stolen my truck and some clothing during the night. That was a problem with allowing a stranger in the cabin and not having a lock on the bedroom door.

That was the last I saw or heard of her. She'd blundered into my life while running from something; she'd stolen my truck to get away. I'd be left with that mystery for the rest of my life. The fate of my vehicle wasn't a mystery. A park ranger came knocking at the cabin door later that day to ask if I'd left it two counties east of there. A sheriff's deputy had located it on the side of a highway, key still in the ignition, but the gas tank dry. The sheriff's office had tracked me down by contacting the police in my hometown and a call placed to my office. My boss had told them where I was and that led them back to the state forest.

The ranger offered to find someone to drive me to where my pickup was impounded and I accepted, not wanting to be stuck without transportation for the rest of my vacation. At the same time, what I'd been through with Cassie — if that really *was* her name — left me wanting to leave the forest preserve and lick my own wounds at home.

So, I packed up and settled my bill at the visitors center and departed with a young man from the Forest Service driving a sedan with government license plates, hoping I'd leave behind the horror and mystery that had come crashing into my life there.

Burnt

Water dripped down on Potsdam as if the clouds were trying to decide whether it was worth fully raining.

Bert Stratton strolled along the elm-lined street. He was scheduled for a meet-up, but made sure to avoid appearing to be in a hurry.

There were many others, both couples and individuals, moving along the pavement. It was clear they hardly enjoyed the chilly, wet afternoon, which reminded Bert of London. Most of the pedestrians used brollies, but Bert wasn't one to hide from the weather.

He was about halfway between the nearest junctions when he spotted the man dressed in all black, casually watching people and vehicles passing him from beneath a black umbrella.

Bert purposefully walked past the man. After another few meters looked ahead of him, then behind him. He turned round and found a seat on the wet bench next to the man he'd come to meet. There were two coffee cups between them on the bench.

'Andrew,' he said quietly in greeting.

'Bert,' the man responded likewise, selecting the nearer of the two cups and handing it to his compatriot. 'A chilly wind blowing in a cruel country ...'

'Unlike the bright sunny days of spring back home,' Bert replied, finishing the code words.

Bert lifted his cup toward his mouth, but Andrew held out a hand to stop him. 'I've rather bad news. Her Majesty is no longer in need of your services.'

The coffee cup lowered, Bert looked sharply at his co-worker. 'What?'

'You're being sacked,' Andrew replied. 'I'd suggest you get your affairs in order.'

Bert's mouth hung open. 'But, why?'

Andrew looked him in the eye. 'Not that I'm authorised to say anything ...' He turned away from Bert. 'but ... Paris.'

The night-club shooting. Bert had been sent in to stop a terrorist cell from attacking people and had got crossed up, missing the terrorists' departure and blowing the mission.

'I'm sorry, Bert. I really am,' Andrew continued. 'Anyone I should pass a message to back in Ealing?'

'No, no,' Bert said bitterly. 'That's already been done. No need to open old wounds.'

'No, 'course not. Enjoy the coffee, last thing you'll get off the Queen's dime.'

Bert hesitantly sipped at the hot, milky beverage. 'Thanks, Andrew. You're a hell of a bloke. Glad you were the one who broke it to me.'

Andrew grunted. 'It's been ... enlightening ... working with you, Bert. Sorry it came to this.'

'Me, too.'

'I must be going. Good luck, though.'

Andrew got to his feet, umbrella in hand, and tipped his hat to Bert before walking off the way Bert had come. Bert took another sip of coffee and suddenly tasted something odd.

Bert rose from the bench and hurried toward his flat, then faltered. His vision swam and his legs refused to obey his brain's commands. He fell and sprawled on the pavement, his coffee spilt next to him.

The people nearby gathered around, but it was too late for any help. Bert's glassy eyes stared blankly at the floor as he released his final breath. The fast-acting poison had done its work, ending his for ever.

The Lost Legions

The 18th Legion marched eastward through the unforgiving landscape of *Germania Superior*.

The skies were dark and rain spit upon us, getting heavier as we marched toward the towering trees. We slowed. The path we followed narrowed dramatically and became a morass of mud.

Once the line moved again, I found myself between two other Legionaries, marching for miles in the cold rain. The path entered a depression between hills.

The whooshing noises just reached my ears before long shafts of spears rained down on us. Dozens of my fellow soldiers collapsed to the ground. I had barely raised my shield before two spears planted themselves into it. There were screams of pain and shouts of anger all around me.

The Legionaries surrounding me put up the shield wall and I dislodged the spears brefore lifting my shield above us, to protect the rest of the line. Once the hail of spears subsided, there came harsh, harrowing shouts of the *Germanii* — they were launching their attack!

I drew my *gladius* and listened. Orders were whispered down the line and we prepared to open the tortoise formation and get ready for battle. The German voices grew louder and louder and the thunder of their feet on the hill agitated many. Finally, the order was given. I pulled down my shield and it fell to the ground.

There were hundreds, thousands of dirty, hide-clad barbarians coming at us, lances and circular shields raised. Pikes broke through shields, killing several around me. I grabbed my fallen shield, struggled to get it upright and heaved it into place in front of me to block the gap where a fellow Legionary had fallen.

The heathen who had skewered him was fighting to pull his lance free of my dying comrade, giving me the chance to stab with all my weight. My sword struck home, its point cutting through the hides meant to protect him. He stumbled back, out of reach.

Another pike came at me, colliding with my helmet with a loud clang. My vision blurred for a moment and I fought to stay on my feet.

Once I could see clearly again, two more barbarians were upon me. I ducked beneath my shield, but their pikes splintered the wood and crossed mere inches from my face. I heaved the shield at them, tying their hands long enough that I could slash and stab. One barbarian's head tumbled down to his feet while the other man collapsed behind him.

As I sized up the next barbarian, I felt a shock in my back. I looked down to see a bloody pike head sticking out of the lower part of my chest. I drew a ragged breath and dropped my sword, falling to my knees as I weakly grasped the weapon protruding from my body.

I looked up just in time to see another barbarian raise his sword over his head and swing it down upon mine. My helmet gave way with a sharp crack as the steel sword dug into my skull. Almost immediately, I felt a warm liquid pour down my head.

I collapsed into the dark, wet muck and knew no more.

John Wesser

John Wesser has been a member of the Fox Valley Writers Group for several years. His contributions are included in several volumes of the Foxtales series and can also be found in other notable publications by the group.

He is a retired naval officer and a Vietnam War era veteran. More recently, he has retired from being a computer networking engineer and entrepreneur. He believes in progressive causes and is an outspoken freethinker. For five years he was the president of a local chapter of Americans United for the Separation of Church and State.

In addition, John has been a member of Toastmaster International *since 2010 and has been presented with its highest level of achievement: the Distinguished Toastmaster (DTM) Educational Award, He remains active in his Toastmasters club - Timely Talkers of North Aurora, IL - where he has served in several club and district officer positions, including as president and Area Director.*

Currently, in addition to being a writer and public speaker, he offers his time as a substitute teacher for several local school districts. He would tell you though that his primary avocation is being dedicated to Laurie, his wife of forty-four years, and a grandfather to his three wonderful grandchildren.

A Reluctant Baker

Every year from about Thanksgiving through New Year's Eve, I'm known around my home as "The Baker." I love having homemade baked goods around this time of year. I'm sure you would agree that the aroma of warm pumpkin pies from the oven, or a good whiff of bread freshly baking and filling your senses, it is akin to being in paradise.

I remember as a kid, my mother would labor for days, if not weeks, making pies, cakes and especially fresh bread for the holidays. So when I got married, I asked my wife if she could do some baking. As I recall, she looked up at me and immediately said, "No way! That's too much work. Store-bought bread and pies are good enough for me." But later, she did say, in her loving manner, that if I really wanted to have some homemade baked goods for the holidays, she would be happy to allow me the use the kitchen.

The curious thing is that I've always hated to cook, and that includes baking. I have this philosophy that if something takes longer for me to cook than to eat it, I don't want it. Nevertheless, I found I had to change my attitude about this, especially when it came to holiday baked goods, for if I didn't make them, no one else was going to do it.

I started off with fresh white bread. It turned out great and my family ate it up – including my wife. She loved it, but not enough to bake it herself.

For years we bought pumpkins for the kids at Halloween. They're relatively cheap around that time. We would make Jack-O-Lanterns with some and others we just put on our doorstep as seasonal decorations. Then a few years ago, it occurred to me that it was a waste to just throw them away afterwards. So before the first frost, I started bringing in the ones the kids hadn't carved up and began making traditional pumpkin pies out of them. It is amazing how many pies you can get out of a relatively small pumpkin and how many recipes you can find on the Internet for other things, such as pies, cakes and cookies. (By the way, I use frozen ready-made pie crusts. After all, I'm not a total glutton for punishment.)

The trick is the proper preparation of the pumpkin. What I do is cut it up into chunks about the size of your hand – this is after scraping out all the stringy innards and seeds. Then boil (or steam) the pumpkin pieces for about 20 minutes. When you can easily poke the meat with a fork, it's done. Be sure not to boil too long otherwise the meat will turn to mush.

Once the pumpkin is soft, you can easily remove it from the skin with a large spoon. I then separate it into two-cup portions. One cup of pumpkin is equal to about 8-9 ounces by weight. Homemade pumpkin pies are also a lot lumpier, which adds greatly to the eating experience. What I don't use right away I measure out into plastic sandwich bags and freeze. You can also clean, bake and salt the seeds for an additional snack.

So next year, I challenge you to stop wasting those Halloween pumpkins and start making yourself a wonderful seasonal treat. Explore, experiment and start living the joys of holiday baking.

My Flying Car

There is certainly no doubt that the zeitgeist of our youth is the most significant time of our lives. It's always been the basis for our views on life. Myself, I am a child of the '60s and my views were formed by the Beatles, the Summer of Love, and particularly – technology. My adolescence consisted of space travel, computers and transistorization. Science Fiction was becoming reality. I used to eat up every word of the "futurists" in Science and Popular Mechanics magazines, and in particular, the promises of someday having a "Flying Car."

It's been fifty frustrating years, and now that I've reached the grand old age of 65, I've only one thing to say ... WHERE'S MY FLYING CAR!

Oh, you must admit I've been patient, while silently following the "molasses in January" progress the industry has been making on my car. Oh, there have been plenty of upstarts like Gilo Industries with their *Parajet SkyRunner* or Beyond Roads with their *Maverick*, and on and on. But, these are all experimental craft that sell in excess of $100,000 or more, not production vehicles!

Okay, to be honest, I've sometimes felt my hopes might just be a fantasy because of the one significant design defect in all our cars – the nut behind the wheel. Many drivers can barely operate their vehicles in two dimensions, let alone three. To operate a Flying Car today, operators would be required to be certified pilots as well as drivers.

But, my friends, as Bob Dylan once said, "The times, they are a-changin'."

Think for a moment about the cell phone sitting in your pocket; a mere ten years ago all you could do was make phone calls and maybe send a text. Ten years before that they had to be physically installed in your car. Now these wireless miracles are full-blown computers with GPS and apps of all kinds.

See a trend here? The machines and functionalities of our daily existence are merging.

Unless you've been living under a rock, you've heard of Google's driverless cars. Many of our new cars have driver-assist capabilities that help you watch out for traffic, and will actually apply the brakes for you in case of an emergency.

This technological convergence may soon allow us to see the Flying Car finally sailing over the horizon. If technology can relieve drivers of the responsibilities of operating their vehicles in a two-dimensional environment, it's only a matter of time before the capability is expanded to the third. We will then see a network of autonomous vehicles appearing in the skies over our heads.

Just think of it; everyone may soon have their own personal robotic chauffeur. Just get in the car and say, "Home, James," and when you wake up you'll be home in your garage, safe and sound, and no more DUI's.

So, I ask again, where's my Flying Car?

On Venturing to Mars

The famous astronomer, Edwin Hubble, after whom the first space-based telescope was named, once said, "Equipped with his five senses, man explores the universe around him and calls the adventure Science."

I remember well fighting hard to stay awake, one Sunday evening in July 1969, while watching a grainy black and white picture on my parent's new color television set as Neil Armstrong came out of the Eagle and climbed down the leg of the LEM to the surface of the moon. It was a momentous day in history and a time when every boy wanted to be an astronaut (and some little girls too).

It was only a few years earlier that Star Trek débuted on television prefacing every episode with the words "… to boldly go where no man has gone before."

For over a century, the minds of young people were set ablaze by the works of Jules Verne and H.G. Wells. Movies and TV gave us the tales of Flash Gordon, Buck Rogers and Captain James T. Kirk.

My space-enthusiast buddies and I were convinced we were on the verge of a new era of discovery, especially after being enticed with movies like the mesmerizing, "2001: A Space Odyssey" and after falling in love with the seductive and enchanting, "Barbarella." And then there were our real-life space heroes: Alan Sheppard, John Glenn and Gordon Cooper, just to name a few.

It was said back then that the first man to set foot on Mars was still in high school. We assumed space exploration was now the norm, but in reality, we were living a fantasy. Once President Kennedy's challenge of putting a man on the moon was accomplished, Congress cut funding, and along with it, our aspirations.

We found more than a vision was needed. We needed to partner with those with power and money, but they had their own agenda called "return on investment."

You may recall Columbus got his money from a couple of Spanish monarchs in exchange for the promise of land and riches.

Similarly, Wernher Von Braun had to offer the potential of world conquest to a mad dictator. Later working for the United States, he helped achieve the first manned lunar landing by delivering a new warhead delivery system to our military during the Cold War.

But what will be the impetus of our next trek into space?

What will it take to persuade the money men to finance these efforts?

You guessed it; more power and riches, along with a supply of cheap labor, whether they are soldiers, factory workers or miners. These may not be the quixotic people of dreams but those who would be willing to put their lives on the line to make the rich richer in exchange for a chance to acquire a small fortune for themselves.

I suppose our next major venture into space may be when the financiers discover the money to be made in mining the solar system, starting with the moon, then the asteroids, and eventually - Mars and beyond.

So I ask you... are we on the precipice of a new Age of Exploration? Is our renewed interest in the latest Star Wars and Star Trek movies a harbinger of things to come? Can we again say the first person to set foot on Mars may be in high school today?

My friends, I have little to counter the argument that it may be cheaper and safer to send out probes to expand our knowledge of the universe. However, I'd rather primarily see them as vanguards in preparing our path to exploration. For generations people have eagerly risked their lives attempting to scale the highest mountains, and descend to the deepest depths of the seas. Why? Because what real sense of accomplishment and adventure is there in dispatching a drone compared to venturing in person and experiencing the wonder of being there.

Finally, let us be guided by the inspiring words of the great 19th century Chicago architect, Daniel Burnham, who declared: "Make no little plans; they have no magic to stir men's blood..."

Memories

"They're all dead."

"What! Who's dead, Grandpa?" As I walked into our dimly lit living room, this wasn't something I was expecting my grandfather to suddenly blurt out.

"John Daly, Dorothy Kilgallen, the whole lot."

"What are you talking about?" I said.

"The people on this TV show," Grandpa replied.

"Okay, yeah, I suppose they are. But if it upsets you, why do you keep watching this channel? You're not going to find much else on it. They're mostly all old black and white reruns. It's called the *Nostalgia Channel* for a reason, you know. What show are you watching?"

"*What's My Line?*"

"It's terribly grainy. That's an old game show from the 50s, isn't it?"

"Actually, Annie, this particular episode is from 1950, well before you were born. I remember watching it when it was new. Most shows were broadcast live back then so the quality of the original broadcasts was much better than these old kinescope recordings. It was one of the first programs on CBS when television first came to this town. I don't know if I ever told you, but before our family got a TV, I used to go over to your grandma's house to watch it – back when we were just dating. Her family was one of the first in town to be able to afford a television set. I believe it was a *Sparton*, if I re-member right. It was a console that included a radio and a turntable built into the cabinet. That was very popular back then."

"Sounds like what we'd call a media center today, except now we include a DVD or Blu-ray player in place of the phonograph."

"I suppose that's true; times have changed."

"Funny thing..." I said as I took a sip of the coffee I had brought in with me. "Last week, my sixth grade class and I were going over prefixes and suffixes. I was citing examples such as *telegraph, television, telephone*, but when I brought up the word *phonograph*, they all stopped and stared at me asking, 'What's a phonograph?' They made me feel

48

real old for a moment."

"Welcome to the club, kid."

"No doubt, things certainly have changed a lot for you, haven't they, Grandpa? We've got a lot of different gadgets these days, so everyone's got a TV now. In fact, many people have a set in every room in their house as well as in their pocket. It's interesting to think, you've seen it all, from black and white to color, to cable and satellite, and now digital and Wi-Fi."

"That's for sure. You've got this big 55-inch screen on your wall here. The set I was talking about a few minutes ago was only a 12-inch. I recall some screens back then that were as small as 5-inches or so. Yes, we've come a long way and now they don't even use those old picture tubes anymore, or tubes of any kind."

"I guess that's what they call progress, isn't it?"

"Progress? Well, that reminds me of a conversation my father and I once had with an old neighbor of ours back in the 60s about this so-called *progress*. Old Mr. Kazanski was his name. He was in his 80s at the time and we were talking about John Glenn and the other astronauts going up in space. Mr. Kazanski told us about how he had once read in the local paper as a kid about the Wright brothers and their flying contraption. He was emphatic about not too many people being impressed at the time. 'What practical value was there riding around in an oversized kite?' the newspaper commented."

"Well, I think aviation has come a long way and has certainly proven its value since then, and so has the space program," I said.

"I'll give you that, Ann," Grandpa replied, "but I tend to feel this television stuff will be the death of us, and the Internet too. It may be fine in moderation, but it numbs the brain and discourages people from thinking, from using their imagination – it's too easy. People don't read any more. Everyday, newspapers are going out of business. Television brought us pictures, which was good, but there were times when the visions we saw on the radio were much better."

"People are still reading, they're just reading on their gadgets. They're reading eBooks and online newspapers. Television has also been a great educational tool," I said.

"I suppose so, but it's also a road to melancholy, reminding us that so many of our old friends and favorite celebrities have passed on, as with this show. But then again, before he died, my father used to say the same thing about old movies he used to watch on TV, films and his Hollywood favorites from the 30s and 40s."

"Yeah, and before that there were photographs, pictures, books and all sorts of other things to remind you," I retorted.

"And recordings. I remember old man Kazanski would describe to us instances when some of the old folks in his time would find it spooky seeing and hearing the voices of dead people coming from old recordings and news reels. I suppose it would be kind of spooky if you think about it from their perspective.

"Yeah, but sometimes I just like to comfortably park myself here, close my eyes, and imagine it is 1951 once again. I visualize myself sitting next to your Grandma, relaxing quietly on her parents' couch the way we used to do and just enjoying each other's company, holding hands, and watching TV."

I noticed Grandpa was now staring back toward the TV but it was more of a thoughtful gaze into space with his lips parted, just a little. A moment later he quietly intoned, "She had such beautiful, soft hands, so lovely, so warm. It was heaven being near her."

After a short silence, Grandpa's attention drifted back to his TV program and I slowly and quietly left the room, leaving him to his memories.

Room of Dreams

As I stand next to my bunk this evening and gaze out my window, I find myself parsing a view I've seen a million times. It's still the unchanging view of an ordinary red-brick wall, but today, after spending two years at this institution, I feel incredibly different. A shadow cast by the setting sun now seems spiritually uplifting.

In the past, I've always found pessimism to be the answer. It has always properly set my expectations. There's no disappointment if there's nowhere to go but up. These past years have been as much a fight for survival as were all the years before--a time of financial uncertainty and academic struggle.

Nevertheless, I must say that today was the most unusual day of my life.

It's hard to believe it's only been a week since graduation day. So much has happened; it almost seems like a lifetime. Back then, sitting in Mason Hall with my fellow classmates, I remember being concerned about my class standing, my final grades and my future prospects. For someone planning on pursuing a Ph.D., I wasn't anywhere near the top, or even in the middle for that matter.

I couldn't help but wonder what I was there and where my life was going. Learning this stuff was harder than I thought it would be, and it wasn't the glamorous and interesting work I imagined it could be. In fact, I found much of it quite tedious and at times downright boring; definitely nowhere to go but up.

Nonetheless, life can't be all work. We must all establish our priorities. I chose South State U. because I understood it was a bit of a *party school*. Well, normally it is, but not with the bunch of stoics in my study group. My fellow grad students were much too serious for my liking and failed to possess the slightest sense of humor. I've yet to see or hear one of them crack a joke (or even smile) in the two years since I first walked on campus. But then again, they're the ones who'll probably be rich and successful by forty (but dead from stress by fifty-five).

I consoled myself by thinking, *hey, expectations!* I just completed my master's degree and that should count for something--you'd think. Anyway, there is no turning back now, not with this load of student debt on my back.

Psycho-cybernetics is a relatively young field. It was founded in the later half of the twentieth century, a little over 50 years ago. So I'm confident I have a good shot at a career - provided I'm able to secure my Ph.D. This requirement is firmly among the minimum demanded in this field to get a decent entry-level position.

In my dorm room a few days ago, I noticed my roommate Billy had a recent copy of the campus newspaper. He left it on the table open to the classifieds page. On it he circled, in red, a vague and strangely worded ad that stated someone was looking for doctoral students who might wish to assist with some "psycho-work" they called *Project X*.

From the ad, I read the guy running the project was some dude named Professor Neuroski. The only contact information in the ad was a school email address. The application deadline was the next day and offered a nice little sum. There was nothing more said about the project or what *Project X* might entail.

I asked Billy if he had applied. "Yes," he said, but also exclaimed somewhat annoyingly that he was turned down. He was a good student (one of those straight 'A' stoics I spoke about) and from a well-known family, so I asked him if he knew why.

"Well," he said, "all they would tell me was they didn't think I had the right 'demeanor,' whatever that means."

"They didn't even give you a hint about what they're looking for?" I said.

"Not really, but I heard a rumor around campus what they're searching for is some odd candidate who's only getting B's and C's. Apparently they're conducting some sort of psycho experiment where they put people in a room and do stuff to their brain."

"What kind of stuff?"

"I don't know. However, I did overhear someone at the Coffee Corral refer to this *Project X* thing as the 'Room of Dreams.'"

"Room of Dreams? That's a strange name."

"Yeah. What I heard is that they plan on inducing all sort of imaginings in your brain with magnets or something; some pleasant but mostly terrifying just to get your reaction. It all sounds sick to me. To tell you the truth, although the money sounded good, I think even if I had been selected, I'd probably decline their offer. Those people over there were plain weird."

Weird? Maybe, but it could also be fun. I thought about it for a moment and concluded that old Billy, being a better student than myself, probably had other offers available to him anyway. Besides, coming from a wealthy family he didn't have any of the student debt loads I did. Plus, the job intrigued me. The pay was good and I seemed to be qualified, at least on one level. Therefore, I immediately got online and applied for the position. *Nothing ventured, nothing gained*, I thought.

I was surprised to get a response to my email not less than ten minutes later offering me an interview that very night. I did find it odd though that the time of the interview was 10:47 p.m. at Albert Hall. That was all the way across campus and I didn't have much time. I quickly jumped into the shower and got dressed. I grabbed my resume, a copy of my transcripts and I was off on my bike. Albert Hall was on the older side of campus and a good distance away, but I made it with two minutes to spare--or so I thought.

Upon my arrival, I hesitated for a minute. I had a nervous stomach. I couldn't help recall that my last several interviews didn't go all that well. But I also knew I needed this job and had few other options. So, I secured my bike, gathered up my courage and scurried to the entrance.

The building was dark except for one lone light I saw burning in a window up on the top floor. I rang the bell and received an answer through a very scratchy-sounding intercom. I heard a woman's voice greet me saying, "Welcome, Mr. Jones. Please proceed to Room 505." This was followed by the buzzing of the door lock. Entering the building and hallway, I was a little annoyed to discover there was no elevator. I had no choice but to hike it up all five floors via the large open stairway.

It was my first time in this building. It must have been well over a hundred years old. Everything smelled musty. Everywhere there was dated architectural décor of brass, olive marble and old wooden trim thickly covered with multiple layers of green and grey paint. The floors creaked, as did the stairs, as I made my way up to Room 505. I found the hallways and stairs dimly lit but sufficient to let me see where I was going. I wondered for a moment if some of the light fixtures still contained their original 25-watt incandescent bulbs from the 1900s. The patterns on the carpet runs were also washed out and worn thin.

It took me several minutes to get up the stairs and upon reaching the fifth floor; I was nearly out of breath. I didn't realize I was that badly out of shape. I thought I'd rest a moment before proceeding, but suddenly a door opened down the hall. Stepping out and standing in the doorway was a beautiful blonde who was roughly my age. She had a striking resemblance to Marilyn Monroe and was wearing a conservative black dress with matching stiletto heels. As she stood there I noticed a large, faded sign next to the door that simply read: "505."

With my leg muscles recovering from their ordeal, I immediately straightened up and began my approach when I heard her say, "Thank you for coming, Mr. Jones. You are late." Before I could respond, she added in an unusual, intriguing accent, "My name is Nasrin; I am Professor Neuroski's assistant. Please, come in and have a seat."

As I followed her into the room, we had only proceeded a few feet when she stopped abruptly and spun around. Surprised, I bumped into her and our lips almost met. Looking deep into my eyes, she confirmed in a low, sultry voice, "The professor will be with you--shortly." She then quickly turned again and slowly walked over towards a table and a couple of chairs that were positioned in the middle of the room. The floor of the old building creaked as she strolled across them before carefully taking her seat behind the table.

All I could think about was how hot she looked in that dress but as I stood there I couldn't help but pay a little attention to the odd collection of equipment scattered about the room. There were racks of what looked like computers and related equipment, a few book-cases, a workbench with stools, and I noticed several unusual bellows-like contraptions as well as other stuff the likes I've never seen before.

Then I heard my name called again, this time by a male voice. I spun around and discovered a distinguished man who looked to be in his 70s. He was a little shorter than me and was wearing an old, out-of-style brown tweed suit with a vest and a red bow tie. I tried to respond but choked a bit, being still enamored by Nasrin.

Uncomfortably, I tried to quickly clear my throat and say, "Ah, yes, yes sir, that's me. Professor Neuroski, I presume?"

"Yes, yes," he said, "come into my office, young man. Would you like some water?"

"Yeah, sure," I said.

"Nasrin, could you bring this gentleman some water, please?" the professor said as we proceeded to his office.

"Yes, Professor, right away" she responded.

Upon walking into his office, we shook hands before he closed the door. I stole this opportunity to lean over and look back to get another glimpse of Nasrin as she got up to retrieve the water. Professor Neuroski then asked me to have a seat.

I sat down on one of the two wooden folding chairs he had available. I then nervously offered my paperwork to the old man. Accepting it, he walked around and sat down in a tattered leather chair behind an old wooden desk. Moving some other papers out of the way, he took a pair of reading glasses out of his jacket pocket and began looking over my credentials. He read and carefully reread my documentation--several times. It was as if he was looking for something in particular.

As I sat there quietly fidgeting, a knock was heard at the door. Nasrin walked in and offered me a small bottle of spring water along with a very provocative smile as she placed her hand gently on my shoulder, giving it a slight squeeze on her way out. I smiled as her short visit helped calm my anxiety. The professor read on and on. As he read, I heard him utter several "a-hum's," as well as a few "ah's," while tapping the eraser of his pencil over a few lines as he read them. He also made a note or two in the margins of every page. Unfortunately, I had no indication whether those were positive or negative utterances. As he read, he swayed and squeaked in his chair. I sat as motionless as I could while sweat trickled down my forehead.

Finally, the professor raised his head, sat back in his chair, and said in a clear Midwestern voice, "Mr. Jones, why are you here?"

Caught a little off-guard at this question I said, "Well, to be quite candid, Professor Neuroski, I did just find your ad this afternoon and I haven't had a lot of time to prepare, but psycho-cybernetics is my chosen field of study and I was intrigued by your ad. I'll admit I'm also not the best student in my class, but I have chosen this field of study because I found it fascinating. I don't know much about your work right now, but I've no doubt its very important. I can assure you I'm a hard worker and will be dedicated to this project. And to be brutally honest, I really need this job. I also must admit, I'm quite curious about what your *Project X* is all about. Can you tell me a little about what you're doing, I mean, about *Project X*?"

Duh, I felt I was rambling on like some adolescent, but was very startled when I heard him blurt out his answer.

"No!" he exclaimed as he tossed his glasses onto his desk.

"That is to say," he continued, "I can't tell you anything about the project right now, but you'll learn more in good time. I like you, Mr. Jones. Actually, I know more about you than you think. I've had my eye on you for awhile and I was hoping you would respond to my ad. I'm glad you finally did. You seem to be just the kind of person I've been seeking, Mr. Jones. If you want the job it's yours, but I need your answer right now."

"Oh, wow! This is incredible! Yes, yes, of course, Professor! Thank you very much, Professor. You won't be sorry."

"As to that, we'll see. But first you'll need to complete your employment paperwork with Nasrin before you leave. You may recall from the ad, the project starts tomorrow.

"One more thing, I'm going to have to ask you to sign a non-disclosure agreement. It's a must. Do you have any objections with that?"

"No, no objection. But of course, Professor; sounds like it must be a *top secret* venture."

"Well, it's something like that. However, I'm quite serious, Mr. Jones. On this project, secrecy and trust will be of the utmost importance. The information with which you will be entrusted cannot be divulged to anyone outside the confidence of our group, and I mean *anyone*."

"Um, yes sir. I understand, sir. You can count on me to keep my mouth shut."

"Good! Nasrin will go over all this with you in more detail. Once you and she have completed all the necessary forms, you may leave, but please be back here by 9 a.m. sharp tomorrow. You'll be working with another associate named Charlotte. She's a very nice young woman who's been with us for a while now."

After a few more niceties, Professor Neuroski led me out of his office, across the crabby old floorboards and over to Nasrin's table. She had all the necessary paperwork ready for me to fill out: both the university and government forms. Lastly, she handed me a form labeled "Non-Disclosure and Authorization Agreement." No doubt this is the form the professor was so hot about.

"This document," Nasrin said, "will be the most-important piece of paper in your file. It holds a lot of legal weight with the professor, so please read and heed it very carefully, then sign it."

As I glossed over the long document, I found it contained a lot of legalese, but I think I got the gist of it. If I didn't live up to this agreement, the professor and the university would come down on my neck with both feet and would make the rest of my life totally miserable. I didn't read every word, but I felt it was worth signing to get this job, no matter how boring it may turn out to be. I just had to do my job and keep my mum about it. So, I went ahead and I signed it, still not having any real idea what *Project X* was all about or exactly what I was getting myself into.

Nasrin then stretched out her right hand and said, "Welcome to the Project X Team, Mr. Jones." I took her hand and we shook for about a minute. I found her hand to be very soft, warm and as beautiful as the rest of her.

"Starting tomorrow," she said, "you'll be working with Charlotte. She is a wonderful woman and I know you two will get along famously. By the way, may we call you 'Jack?' We're a small friendly group here and prefer using each other's first names."

"I wouldn't have it any other way."

"Wonderful," she intoned with that mystery accent of hers.

"And the professor?" I asked.

"Oh, to us he is strictly 'Professor,' Jack."

"But of course," I said, respectfully.

"I have a little more work to do before I lock up. You can find your way out, yes? Are there any further questions before you leave?'"

"Actually, yes. Before I go, can you please tell me where you're from? I love your accent."

"I'm Persian," she said with a smile.

"Interesting. Thank you and good night, Nasrin."

"Goodnight, Jack."

Persian! I said to myself going down the stairs. *Not bad.*

I easily found my way out and back to my bike. I was much lighter on my feet going down that long stairway than I was going up, and I didn't mind the musty odor anymore. In fact, it now smelled sweet and comforting.

The next morning the air was much cooler and drier than it was the previous evening. A front had moved through during the night, and I was in a great mood, so it was a beautiful morning. I arrived a bit early knowing I had that long flight of stairs to contend with and I didn't want to walk in late again. Nor did I wish to have everyone see me all out of breath. It occurred to me an added benefit of this job might be the exercise I'd be getting every day from those stairs. One does have to think positive. (My attitude was definitely changing.)

When I arrived once again at Room 505, Nasrin and the Professor were absent. Instead, there was another young woman present sitting on a stool at the workbench wearing a long white lab coat. She had her back to me as I entered the room. When she heard me she quickly turned around and smiled. She then slid off her stool and walked over towards me. As she approached it occurred to me that the floor was not creaking under her feet. *Wow*, I thought to myself, *even this old building is happy with this incredible day.*

As she came closer, my eyes were totally fixed upon her. She was simply gorgeous. She possessed a goddess figure that could stop an army in its tracks. I thought for a moment, *the professor can sure pick 'em.*

Her lab coat was open and I could plainly see she was wearing a bright yellow dress, very short with spaghetti straps and a plunging neckline that was quite revealing. It was also made of a very thin material and molded itself very effectively to her well-endowed body. Disappointingly, I also noticed a diamond and wedding ring on her left hand.

"You must be Jack," she said as she reached out to shake my hand. "Good morning, I'm Charlotte."

"Oh, yes, good morning, Charlotte. Where is everyone?" I asked as we walked back over to the workbench. We each took a seat on the stools.

"The professor is teaching a class this morning, and Nasrin had to run an errand, so it's just you and me for at least an hour," she said in a sultry voice while gently touching my hand.

"Okay, ah… so what's the plan for today?" I said while trying to keep my composure. Her bedroom eyes were powerfully attention-grabbing, to say the least.

"Well, we could start by going over some of the aspects of *Project X*. As you know, psycho-cybernetics is based upon setting goals, both inner and outer goals."

"Yes, I know," I said sheepishly, "and visualizing a positive outcome."

"Wouldn't it be nice," she said while once again sliding off her stool and sliding her hand briefly across my leg, "if we started by setting a positive goal of getting to know each other a little better."

She then took off her lab coat and when she did, one of the spaghetti straps of her dress fell over her right shoulder in a provocative manner. She dropped her coat over her stool, and then looked at me with her sky-blue eyes and a salacious smile.

She was incredibly desirable and I wanted to take her into my arms that moment, but again I saw the rings on her finger and said, "But aren't you married?"

"Oh, yeah, but it's over between us. We're in the process of getting a divorce."

I couldn't believe this was happening to me and for a moment, I thought I had died and gone to heaven. But then the door to the office burst open and in walked a burly guy, six-foot two, at least 250 pounds and very angry.

Startled, Charlotte pushed herself away from me and repositioned her dress strap back up onto her shoulder. While reaching for her lab coat she yelled at the man, "Tony, what are you doing here?"

"Never mind that, what the hell is going on here?" he retorted. Then while motioning his right hand towards me, he added, "And who's this dude?"

"He's my new lab partner. What's it to you, you big oaf?"

Now turning his attention towards me, Tony shouted, "What do you think you're doing with my wife?"

"Your wife!" I exclaimed, knowing we were in a bit of a rather compromising position.

"I've had enough of your cheating, you little bitch!" Tony said heatedly.

Everything was happening very fast, and before I could say anything else, Tony reached into his waistband and produced a 9-mm automatic pistol and began shooting wildly at both Charlotte and myself.

"Hey, hey!" I shouted while holding up my hands.

The first shot hit a lamp behind me, and the next shattered the window. With the third shot I heard Charlotte scream and everything went dark.

I now found myself scared out of my wits. *"Oh, my God,* I thought, *am I dead?"* I don't recall losing consciousness, but I was in the dark and surrounded by an unnerving silence. I didn't know where I was and my anxiety skyrocketed. My heart raced and I began to shake uncontrollably with the thought that I might really be dead. Then, I felt a cool, gentle breeze at my back which served to calm my nerves and granted me a more tranquil feeling. Tiny specks of light began to appear which were gathered up and driven like fallen leaves in autumn by the waft of air I was feeling. Slowly, they got brighter and increased in number and velocity. They swirled and merged into a vortex ahead of me as I found myself also being caught up in the flow and dragged along. As they congregated into a larger and larger spot of light ahead, I started to notice several silhouettes moving about within the tunnel of light. As I got closer, I heard the shadowy figures speaking something to each. Their bold voices echoed like being in a cathedral.

Finally, I was able to discern the voice of one who came forward and spoke distinctly in an authoritarian voice, "Shall he be judged?"

Is this guy referring to me? I thought.

"No!" I heard another reply. "He is not of us."

"Return him from whence he came," demanded another.

"It shall be done," replied the first figure.

Immediately, complete darkness fell over me once again. As my sanity slowly reemerged, I found myself standing alone in the middle of Room 505, next to the table where Nasrin and I had sat the night before. Remembering the incident that seemed to occur just moments before when I was here with Charlotte and Tony, I immediately ran my hands over my chest and looked over my body: no bullet holes, no blood, no anything. I appeared to be okay. *So what the hell just happen to me*, I wondered--*a dream, a hallucination?*

Then I heard the sound of the cranky old floor squeak once again. Turning around, I saw Professor Neuroski walking towards me from his office. He stopped, pulled up a chair and asked me to sit down. I complied although still stunned from the experience. Then he did the same.

"How do you feel, Jack?" he asked.

"I don't know, Professor. Am I ... was I ... dead?" I asked.

"No, no. Far from it, my boy."

"I'm confused, Professor, what the hell just happened to me? I don't understand."

"Please, just relax, Jack. You did well. You were just initiated into *Project X*. Did it seem real enough to you?"

I abruptly sat up straight in my chair. "Real enough? Wait! You mean it wasn't?" I said shockingly. I then turned my body to survey the room and asked, "What happened to Charlotte?"

I was sure the professor was only referring to the part where I thought I died and had experienced some form of transcendence into an afterlife.

"Let me explain, Jack. You're familiar with the TV show, *Star Trek*, are you not?

"Ah, yeah, of course. I've seen it," I said squirming in my seat and still unsettled from the experience.

"I'm specifically referring to the follow-on series they called *Star Trek: The Next Generation* where they introduced the concept of a *holodeck?*"

"Yeah, sure. What about it?"

"This room has been configured in a similar manner. It's kind of an experimental holodeck. Sorry to put you through all that without any kind of warning or preparation, but technically, if you read it thoroughly, it was covered in the agreement you signed. This demonstration was necessary to observe and obtain an honest and true assessment from you. Your encounter with Charlotte, Tony and the afterlife incident that followed were all holographic simulations. None of it actually happened in real-life.

I couldn't believe my ears. "You're kidding me! *None* of it happened!"

"It was essentially a projection into your mind, Jack."

"This is absolutely incredible. It certainly was real to me; very, very real."

At this point I had to get out of my chair and walk around a bit. The shock of it all was still fresh and I felt I needed to walk it off a bit and take in a few very deep breaths.

"This technology is powerful in that via my brain-computer interface, it offers an enhanced mental experience. You can think of it as combining virtual reality with artificial intelligence."

"But I have to know, what about Nasrin? Is she real?"

"Oh yes, she's quite real: fully flesh and blood. She'll be back in the office on Monday. She's anxious to get to know you better too. And by the way, I'm sure you'll be pleased to know that she's not married.

"However, Jack, the question is, are you still willing to work with us on this project? The potential of this technology, as you can imagine, is great. But before I will release it to the world, I not only need to ensure that the technology is rock solid, but that the public has been prepared, educated and will be protected. It needs definitive fail-safes built-in to prevent abuses.

"In my elite team, I need someone with a good understanding of psycho-cybernetic theory and applications, but not purely from an academic sense. I need a street-wise individual closer to the real world to monitor and keep vigil during the development of this project and beyond. We'll need to be proactive with solid legal and ethical policies, arguments for its use, as well as proposed regulatory legislation for lawmakers.

We discussed yesterday this being a *top secret* type of project. Once the word gets out, it'll only be a matter of time before the governments and the militaries of the world will be descending upon Room 505. We must be prepared. As you can see, we've got a lot of work ahead of us.

"This will be a significant endeavor, but also a ground-floor opportunity for the right people who are willing to dedicate their lives to it. So, what do you say, Jack, interested in a challenging ride?"

"Wow, this is a lot to take in at one time, but I see your point, Professor. After having experienced this first hand, I can appreciate its potential for good, evil and everything else across the spectrum.

"This certainly is a landmark day for me, Professor, as well as for the whole world, I suppose. If I may say so, I see this as a turning point in science and engineering, and I'd be crazy not to want to be a part of it.

"So yes, without a doubt, Professor, I'm onboard. I wouldn't pass this up for the world. Thank you for considering me."

"I'm very glad to hear you say that, Jack. I know you won't be regretting this decision."

"So where do we go from here, Professor?"

"Well, young man, I believe there's nowhere to go but up."

Dolores Whitt Becker

Dolores Whitt Becker was born and raised in Wisconsin and settled in Batavia after a couple of decades of more or less aimless wandering. In addition to writing, she has been a music student, an artists' model and an actor, while occasionally holding a 'real' job too dull to mention. When she was hired by the public library, she finally knew what she wanted to be when she grew up. She was 34 at the time. She has been married and divorced, had two children and lost one of them. Her first professional publication was in the premier and, as it turned out, only issue of Mountainland Magazine. As a member of the Fox Valley Writers Group, her work has appeared in Foxtales 3 & 4 *and* Phantasms' Door. *Her second professional sale was to the recent ghost story anthology* Familiar Spirits, *edited by Donald J. Bingle and William Pack. All of these publications can be checked out from the Batavia Public Library, and all but the first can be purchased through Amazon.com. Dori Becker now lives in Roselle but still works in Batavia and maintains her ties to the Fox Valley area.*

Author's Note:
Poe and parody were significant features of my upbringing, so it was probably inevitable that at some point I would bring the two together. Fun fact: I wrote the first draft of The Penguin by hand, with a sprained thumb on my dominant hand, barely able to grip the pen and alternating with my off hand when my thumb got too sore. Couldn't say which produced the worse handwriting… db

The Penguin

Once, upon a mead, knight-leery while I pounced the weak, unwary,
Prowled for any a coin or curious bauble of forge-wroughten ore –
While I counted, neatly stacking, suddenly there came a thwacking
As of sword-sheath gently smacking, smacking against chain armor.
"'Tis some traveler," I stuttered, "walking on the moonlit moor.
Only this, and nothing more."

Indistinctly I remember, it was in the meek September.
Knowledge of my strength and limber fought the fear-spawned rising gorge.
Eagerly I wished an arrow, vainly had a sought a barrow,

Where to hide until the morrow – for I had no weapons stored;
Searched the pair I late had preyed on for a blade of any sort,
Dagger, polearm, axe or sword.

And the breezes, bold, unbidden in the grass where I lay hidden
Scared me, dared me not to lie there, skulking, sodden, stiff and sore.
So that now, to slow the greying of my hair, I lay there, praying:
"'Tis some reveler a-straying drunken, unarmed, 'crost the moor,
Some rich traveler who treks unwary 'crost the moonlit moor.
Gods, be with me, I implore!"

Presently, my bowels tightened; slowly I became less frightened.
"Gods," prayed I, "or Devils, truly your assistance I implore!
For, the fact is, I am craven; here I have such meager haven.
This faint heart, I beg you, braven; let me stand, and cringe no more.
I am scarce prepared – so be it." Here I stood, and faced the moor
– Darkness there, and nothing more.

Slow into the tall grass sinking, long I lay there, peering, thinking,
Sweating, swearing oaths no mortal ever thought to swear before.
But my nerves remained unmended, still my loot remained untended,
And my way to town, unwended, back across the lonely moor.
This I pondered, and the wind disturbed the grasses as before
– Merely this, and nothing more.

Back unto my booty turning – still my wretched entrails churning –
Soon again I heard a smacking, somewhat louder than before.
"Surely," thought I, "surely I will not for very long be able
To stay hidden in this stubble. This time, I am toast, for sure.
Let my guts be still a moment, I this misery deplore!
'Tis a rich monk, nothing more."

Boldly, then, I made to rumble when, with many a squawk and stumble,
Up there stepped a motley Penguin, of the white Antarctic shore.
Not the least endearing looked he, not a moment paused or took he
When, with mien of shark or bookie, lurched across the windswept moor,
Lurched up to and sat upon my pile of sweet, ill-gotten ore,
Lurched and sat, and nothing more.

Then, this ugly fowl beseeching my mad fancy into speeching
By the stupid, curious wonder in the countenance it wore:
"Though thy wings be limp and fruitless, if thou meanst to leave me lootless,

By these feet, unshod and bootless, thou shalt fly across the moor!
Tell me why I shouldn't simply kick thy butt from off my hoard."
Quoth the penguin, "Furthermore..."

Much I marveled, this ungainly fowl to hear request so plainly
That I tell him further of my plan to get him off my store.
For I could not help but wonder, having heard my plan to sunder
His foul butt from my fair plunder, he would have me tell him more.
When a man is told that he will soon be battered, bruised and sore,
Does he answer, 'Furthermore?'

But the penguin, squatting fatly on the pilfered pile, spoke flatly
That one word, though I a stream of choice invective did outpour.
Nothing further then he spouted, simply sat and stared and pouted
Till I scarcely less than shouted, "Other thieves have come before!
In a moment, I shall trounce thee, as I trounced the ones before!"
Quoth the penguin, "Furthermore..."

Startled by reply repeated after my outburst so heated,
"Mayhap," mused I, "what it utters is its only stock and store,
Caught from some pontificator, some unmerciful debater,
Or just some unceasing prater, some unshutupable bore,
One whose every thought or statement that continuation wore
Of 'Further – furthermore'."

But, the penguin now annoying my mad fancy into toying
With the notion of him slowly roasting like a spitted boar
– So, upon the wet grass sitting, I betook myself to pitting
Method against method, hitting on no way to do the chore.
For I had no knife to gut him, nor a flame to roast him o'er,
And, to quote him, furthermore,

While I was engaged at cooking, who knows who might, chance, be looking,
Who might spot the fire that I thought to turn the penguin o'er?
This and more I sat debating, with my hunger not abating,
And the Penguin dumbly waiting on the pile I'd gloated o'er,
On the pile of booty those two, rank and stiff upon the moor,
They shall press, ah, nevermore!

Then methought to drive him squawking not by fighting but by talking –
Repetitious ravings on the reason why I haunt the moor.
"Look," spake I, "whatever power sent thee to my meager bower

At this grim, ungodly hour, let me tell thee what it's for.
Let me tell thee why I wait to rob alike the rich and poor."
Quoth the Penguin, "Furthermore..."

"Profit!" said I. "Worldly riches! Profit, still, in fens and ditches!
Whether in a prince's palace or a sad and storming moor,
Money is the only answer! Whether ye be knave or lancer,
Greed's the tune and ye, the dancer; what ye have, ye must have more!
Gold's the king of every kingdom, lord of every peopled shore!"
Quoth the Penguin, "Furthermore..."

"Profit!" said I. "Coinage golden! Profit, still, if earned or stolen!
That is all, there is no further! Hear me, bird, there is no more!
By the gold which is my master, if thou touch but one piastre
Of that pile, thine alabaster belly will be ripped and tore!
They will find thy mangled carcass rotting on the musty moor!"
Quoth the Penguin, "Furthermore..."

"Let that be our word of parting, motley fowl!" I hissed, upstarting.
"Get thee back into the tempest, and the blighted, windswept moor!
Leave no dropping on my plunder, get thee back into the thunder!
There, let thee be ripped asunder, else I do it here for sure!
Take thy snoot from out my face and get thy butt from off my hoard!"
Quoth the Penguin, "Furthermore..."

– And the Penguin? Coins to cobbles, still he wobbles, still he hobbles
'Round the paltry pile of plunder on the melancholy moor.
As for me, I robbed another, some incautious Roman brother
– Having neither mate nor mother, made my home a tavern floor.
And my soul, from out this tavern, owned by my chief creditor,
Shall be lifted, nevermore.

May, 1986

The Ray-Gun

Once upon a mid-flight bleary, while I blundered, thick with theory,
Overlooking a spate of spurious readings from the data store –
While I plodded, past complaining, suddenly there came a whining
As of engines' sudden straining – straining at the load they bore.
"'Tis some officer," I muttered, "whistling past my cabin door –

Only this and nothing more."

Ah, the scan of the penumber, it was there in black and amber,
Where each scintillant, glowing number sought to toast my eyeballs sore.
Wearily I watched the readout, mainly I had thought to weed out
From this hash, coherent feedout – feedout on the meteor –
Of the rare and radiant mineral which was simply called 'The Ore' –
Nameless fancy, heretofore.

And the varied, vast evasion lurking in each wrong equation
Mocked me, blocked me with statistic errors never found before;
So that now, to ease the aching of my head, that search forsaking
"There's some officer out making music in the corridor –
Some drunk officer out making music in the corridor; –
This, instead, I will explore."

Presently my headache faded, once I had the pain out-waited,
"Sir," said I, "whoever's out there, I do not your sound ignore;
If I held back from responding, when I heard your song resounding
It's because my head was pounding – pounding like the rod of Thor –
Now it's better, and I'll join you" – here I slid aside the door: –
Empty was the corridor.

Mirrored in the stainless plating, long I stood there watching, waiting,
Harking, hearing hums no mortal ear had ever heard before;
For the sound was quite inhuman, nor did any light illumine
Either officer or crewman; baffled, "What the Hell!" I swore.
This I whispered, and an echo carried down the corridor
Merely this, and nothing more.

Back into my room rebounding, all my blood within me pounding,
Soon I heard again a whining, somewhat shriller than before.
"Ah-ha!" said I, "Revelation! Something's in the ventilation.
I'll just make a quick summation, for the maintenance report;
I'll just call right down this minute, and to Maintenance report –
There's a problem, of some sort."

There and then I flipped the toggle, when, my tired brain to boggle,
In there strode a Mark III Ray-Gun, of the Automated Corps.
Not a human visage wore it, not a bit could I ignore it,
But, instead, did well deplore it, for its noise my eardrums tore,
For the whine of rusty gears that through my skull a hole did bore,

And my headache thus restore.

Then, this robot scourge unspeaking, my nerve endings fairly shrieking
From the constant onslaught of the rude, resounding, raucous roar –
"Though you may be large and deadly, I will meet my maker gladly
Rather than go deaf and madly writhe upon my cabin floor!
Tell me what the hell you're doing here, and quickly, I implore!"
Quoth the Ray-Gun, "Get the Ore!"

Stunned, I staggered back in wonder, thus to hear its voice like thunder
Telling me to do what was already my chief – only! – chore.
Could they think, our fearless leaders (soulless slugs and bottom-feeders!)
I was one of those unheeders, who their ordered tasks ignore?
Did I need to be reminded, by this metal-masked horror
That I had to find The Ore?

But the Ray-Gun, standing rigid, with its voice inhuman frigid
Said no more, though now its screeching seemed less strident than before.
Nothing further then it uttered, while I mused and mulled and muttered,
Swore at it, and finally stuttered, "Is that all you came here for?
If that's all you have to tell me, go, and let me do my chore!"
Then the thing said, "Get the Ore!"

Rattled by this repetition, from this creature of perdition,
"Maybe," thought I, "there's a problem in this robot's program store.
Could be, there's a chip that going, or a circuit close to blowing,
I have no real way of knowing, it might have a faulty core.
Maybe that is why is stands here, telling what I knew before
To get it – get the Ore!"

But the Ray-Gun, now advancing on me, its red eye-ports dancing,
Leveled at me its main weapon, blunt of shaft and smooth of bore.
Then, into my desk-chair sinking, in its meager cushion shrinking
Scarcely capable of thinking, thus I faced the predator –
Wond'ring how it thought, when I was paralyzed with stark terror,
I could find that stupid Ore.

There I sat, unmanned and shaking, and my reason near forsaking
As the thing its wicked weapon pointed at my very core.
This was all I could envision – that with mindless, mad precision
It would fry me to a smidgen, smoking blob upon the floor.
Just a stinking, sticky blob, whose chances then to find the Ore

Would be lost forevermore.

Then I thought its aim did waver, troubled by some inner quaver
Sent by circuitry whose functions triggered some doubt in its core.
"Shit!" I swore, "my god, who sent you? What malfunction now has bent you
To this task? I do resent you charging in here like a boar,
Telling me, as if I didn't know, what my whole job is for!"
Quoth the Ray-Gun, "Get the Ore!"

"Stop it!" said I, "go away, now! You have come, you've said your say, now!
Whether you were sent, or wandered here by some random error,
Reasonless, yet all enraging, in this senseless act engaging
And my very work upstaging as you tell me what it's for,
Is there, is there any purpose left, that you have come here for?"
Quoth the Ray-Gun, "Get the Ore!"

"Stop it!" said I, "don't remind me! So I toiled, till you did find me!
By that weapon in your arm, that our sage leaders so adore,
By my tortured eardrums ringing, by my eyeballs, red and stinging,
Tell me, just what aid you're bringing, so to help me with my chore!
Will you put that down, and help me analyze the meteor?"
Quoth the Ray-Gun, "Get the Ore!"

"Let that be the last I hear it!" now I roared, restored of spirit.
"Get the hell away, go jump into the drive's plutonium core!
Leave no scratches on my decking, leave the solitude you're wrecking,
Leave me to my lonely trekking, through the data I explore!
Take that gun from out my face, and take those boots from off my floor!"
Quoth the Ray-Gun, "Get the Ore!"

And the Ray-Gun, ever creaking, still is speaking, still is speaking
Those three words, no matter how I beg, or threaten, or implore
But it seems, now, to be straining, so its power must be waning
Soon, it must be – soon! – refraining, silenced, then, forevermore.
And my soul, within that silence, shall my sanity restore –
Maybe, then, I'll find that Ore.

October, 1994

Astrid E. L.

Astrid E.L. is passionate about poetry and has a new fixation with nonfiction. By submitting her poem "Fume" to Waubonsee Community College's literary magazine Horizons, *it sparked an old flame to get the poet back into writing. She served as a contributor once more to the magazine with her work "The Passing Love Note to Eliot," and also as co-editor-in-chief for the 2016 edition of* Horizons.*

Commuting from her small home in Geneva, Illinois, she now makes the journey all the way to Dekalb, Illinois to continue her education at Northern Illinois University; there she will be working on a Bachelor's Degree in English.

Lilacs Outside the Window

Always carried with me is a wonder.
It comes upon me while standing at the kitchen sink,
admiring through the window the pure, cool color of the lilacs.

Never late for spring, but too short lived—poor lilacs.
What, in my power, can I do to extend their bloom, I wonder.
The more I think about fixing a problem, the more my heart will
sink.

My time is used wisely, not being a statue at the sink.
Let my eyes and fingers and nose, especially, enjoy the visiting lilacs;
for that duration of the sniff and touch and scenery settles my wonder.

The wonder will always return; however, my heart will not sink while
I enjoy the lilacs.

The Red Bird Family

On a crisp April morning with blue sky and a cheeky rising sun
I kept still at the kitchen window, pressing as close as I could get
as if I was staring at a diamond ring in display.
I watched a trio of birds, plump cardinals that vacation in my oak

tree.

The proud parents of a new hick.

She held no vivid crimson like her father;

She instead shows the warm, earthy tones of her mother.

Pesky and curious, she followed the red bird throughout the yard;

Identifying various insects squirming in the dirt.

Just as my father and I did, when the world was once, to me, new.

On spring days, when the mother flew away.

Continuing an Absence

My heart was aching, and my mind was spinning around the same drab thoughts—one overlapping the other. That whole afternoon I was trying to extinguish flare-ups from aged feelings; old emotions from a person who got under my skin. She always had me scratching and tearing into myself.

I scratch until it hurts, and until my eyes redden and become glassy. From there I let my misery be known by deliverance of a cracked voice, that being the first step to my recovery from the sadness. Reassurance comes after, and then numbness. Like any proper ouroboros, it doesn't stop there, it only waits until the next turn.

That day differed. I was keeping quiet so that I could ignore my feelings; by doing this I thought I could control my overloaded thoughts. Yet they somehow would leak into my eyes as tears, my lips as a frown, and slump my whole demeanor. That day my discontent showed in the solitude of my person—my reflection in the truck's window capturing my long and drawn stare, despite being blinded by the sun of an August morning. Being that I was with my dad that day, the only person who knows me well, he could see it. With the situation I was in, he once felt like this before. He always said that I wore my heart on my sleeve, and by now it's tattooed on my arm. That day the tattoo ink was fresh again, and my hurt heart was getting re-touched.

We pulled into the loading section of Menards, having to pick up a few sheets of drywall. I asked my dad to tell me about the last time he saw his father. I know this story, and there are times I catch myself reconstructing the scene. I see my dad as a young man, back in the '70s, with his hair of golden fleece, a plain t-shirt and jeans for his attire, walking into a gas station. He could be paying for gas or picking up a green pack of KOOL in a box. Whatever he's buying, his task is interrupted by the presence of his father, a man he had very little contact with throughout his teenage years; imagine the coincidence of running into his own parent at a random gas station. I always imagined my dad smiling like a Cheshire cat while saying "Hey, Pop!" to his father, being genuinely happy to see him. As for his father, my grandfather, I always had to be artistic when conjuring his person. Since my grandfather died before I was born, there's one picture of him that I use to aid my imagination. A dark-haired young man, kneeling on the grass holding a baby—my father—on his knee and they're stationed before a farmhouse in a black-and-white photo that dates from around 1958. I imagine that man giving my then twenty-one-year-old father a puzzled look while asking "Do I know you?"

By then we were just sitting put in the Ford, Dad didn't once reach for the truck's door handle to open it. My dad was slouched comfortably the whole time in the driver's seat, having lit up a cigarette as soon as we parked—he knew we weren't going inside Menards just yet, not while he was telling his story. He told me that he had no regrets about not seeing his father, not even when his dying day came.

Dad knew what was on my mind because I have the same situation he had. For most of my teenage years I had very little contact with my mother, Lisa. A few days prior I agreed to meet her for coffee since she was in town. This meet-up wasn't for business. It wasn't court-ordered, it wasn't at her house or my dad's house, it wasn't in a therapist's office—it was just at a coffee shop, and no one was twisting my arm to see her. My curiosity was all for setting up this coffee date. I wanted to see Lisa in a different light.

Dad told me, while flagging down a heavily chipped blue cart, that he meant to ask about my time with Lisa. He also didn't want to say anything about me going in the first place. He kept quiet and let me do what I wanted to do. I knew what I was getting into, and I was prepared for the emotional drain I always felt as the aftermath from interacting with her. Even with the preparedness, I kept telling myself that this time she won't affect me. No longer an angry young girl, I can handle my thoughts, feelings, and my mother like a reasonable adult.

Lisa and I hugged as soon as I set down my purse at the table she claimed for us. I used to come up to her chest when we embraced, and the gaping absence of time had my grip around her much weaker. It also had me much taller—at least to her chin. She had grown too. Her slim face traced with deep lines around her mouth, eyes, and forehead and my face had become more defined, with cheek bones and clearer skin. She had just retired from the U.S. Post Office, and I completed my associate's degree. I never thought of my mother ever becoming old, and I can't even think about what she thought of me.

Over cappuccinos we caught up the best we could. I didn't go into much depth besides the fact I was finishing community college and starting at Northern Illinois University. She told me about her move with her boyfriend. She recited a few things she read from my Facebook to guide the conversation, taking some interest in my writing; being glad to hear about the path I'm setting myself on with it. We talked about her mother, gossiped about Brian Bemis of Bemis Auto, and why she was in Elburn, one of her childhood towns.

Mundane adult talk; essentially, I was talking to one of my dad's old friends—reaching the best I could at any topic to keep a flow and impress his long-forgotten companion. Eventually I gave up. As soon as my cappuccino was nothing but milky foam at the bottom of my cup, I wanted to get on with my day. I wanted to go home and wait for the ouroboros to tighten within its coil and squeeze out the melancholy that was supposed to be suffocated. Yet I stayed a bit longer that cloudy July afternoon, the curiosity had to get its fill. I was extending what it could hold.

Dad curved the truck around the Menards parking lot to get to an exit, having Skippy's be our next stop for lunch. I confessed to him that I was unsure if I wanted to see Lisa ever again. I thought I made up my mind in the café, avoiding any indication of future meet-ups. I said I would be busy with school and work, or that I'd see about retrieving a footlocker of my old belongings she had. The reasons I gave were valid, but a "no" was never given.

My father didn't agree nor disagree, he brought up what he said before about having no regrets. This time he added, while scooping up a blob of ketchup with two salty fries, that he wouldn't want me having any regrets. He was hinting that I shouldn't be so quick to decide right then and there.

Sitting in public next to my mother brought on a thimbleful of joy. I wondered if any other people in the café observed us, guessing how the older woman and younger woman knew each other. Our dark hair and tan skin was a dead giveaway to our blood relations; look any closer, the black oval beauty marks at the bases of our necks sealed the undoubtable question that I'm her child.

In the same breath of telling him that there was an eagerness, nothing was felt. Not quite a waste of time, but I always end up shaken in my core somehow. It's physical, the tension clasping the bottom of my ribcage, and a weight pressing against my chest. My mind winds up in a completely different universe—molding into the person with the achy heart.

The woman I was talking with that day was the same person I left when I was thirteen: hollow. I'd rather she be an enigma, as I've known her best. Quietly sitting off to the side eating just a bowl of rice; leaving before sunrise for work, and sleeping away Sunday afternoons; cutting off contact from the family every Mother's Day. She who took a steak knife to carve rigid circles into a wall of our living room. When the gifted violets planted by the walkway weren't crushed enough, she had to light them on fire to properly end them. We, my sister and I, starved with her, having our bodies scathed and our emotions blackened by Lisa's lies. Cold as a statue of Medusa, and just as still. That was my mother. I can't decipher who it really was in the café telling me she loved me.

My words started to lessen, and sentences ending in mumbles. Was dad still listening? I recycle the spiel about Lisa so many times that even I get tired of hearing myself. I still rolled around the idea of not seeing her again, of hiding away emails she sends and mentioning little of her. The anger turned to apathy, making my feelings towards her more bearable, yet still mind-numbing. I sighed, instantly validating my dissatisfaction with the whole day; giving the ouroboros another small turn.

I wouldn't wish this wild child of a feeling on anyone. All of that preparation, the mental build-up it botched its protection of me yet again. My curiosity got its satisfaction, and I got to see how grown I've really become with both of my parents witnessing my maturity of handling the family dynamic we have.

Dad got out of the truck after parking it in an alleyway—it continued to gently rumble. He instructed me to get into the driver's seat, giving me control of the Ford Ranger to slip it into the garage back-end first—with him as my guide to make sure I didn't bump into anything.

The Inner Dialogue of an Imbalanced Libra

Is this another bad time?
two people inhabit one body
twirling, in a unison fashion, the same soul
feeling the same heart bleed and the same skin rise in goose bumps
watching the same world with the same eyes
one answers, "Yes" and the other, I don't know."
Is this the making of something scary?
being too comfortable with relapse
consuming too much too fast
getting too cool with endings—everlasting endings
reread the last page, over and over, but it will not change what was written
instead, flip the world, down a snowy hill, and watch it wreck
think about it and
pass it off with a smile, because heaven knows we are our mothers' children
one, with a shaken core and the cold frontal lobe numbness
stutters out, "Stop!" and the other says, "Perhaps."
How long is temporary?
pushing just over 22 years
13 days
1 regretful morning
365 chances in a year
2 people continue to wait quietly
before continuing
Is there such thing as stopping?
one hesitates before failing to answer and the other says, "You tell me."
"Old habits die hard," the other points out
"Too much emphasis is put on the death rather than the haunt."
The other continues:
"Rather than the thing that lightly lingers,
reminiscing everything what once was, and wondering about everything
    that will be.
Rounding about in a perfectly full circle,
and, once complete, will be at the ready to spin again."
Is that a good enough answer?

one body, a map of thousands of paths
some of which have been traveled and
many that have yet to be found
and others that hold "No Trespassing" signs
millions of footsteps printed by two souls
footprints which, every so often, stray away from the paths
one says, "Yes" and the other, "I'm glad you agree."

Empty Day

Nowhere bound,
nowhere bound.

I sit at my desk reading articles about what is happening
They make a discovery, a guy won the lottery, another crafted a
   masterpiece
Just with his bare hands in his living room

How would he fit a canvas between two sofas and a table?
Would he prop it against the TV and the stand-up stereo?
His paints would be lost to clutter, his canvas victim to cats
He could clean it up, fix it up, to only have something else knocked down
And he too will go down, crashing on the couch
In a slouch, pressing remote buttons
Until the TV bursts into color, blaring laughter from the screen
There are girls in "volumized curls," boys brag about their expensive toys

He's flipping through commercials, his disgust never falters
They're selling him Viagra, coaxing him to watch a show
News cameras are out, another attack in Chicago

By now he's stiff as a board, he's over-bored
Too hot for a blanket, but he'll shield himself anyway to take a snooze

So that he can lose
The aches in his body, the pains in the brain
The forgotten day, the wasted youth
the existence of motivation, and lack of food in the fridge
He'll lose sense of morality, the worry of mortality
His sight, his taste, his hearing
The couch, the room, his house, while he lies in place

With a lady who lost her dress, a lady he'll never talk to
He'll lose all recollection
He'll lose him and her and the break in his reality

The clock is striking midnight, the clock is ticking away from midnight

He holds his pulsing head, his feet never felt so heavy
Shuffle through the house, crawl into bed, trip back into the break

Then he'll wake up and venture to the kitchen for his cup, and fill it half
    way up with coffee,
morning's certainty
He will sit and sip at his desk, get a chuckle from the funnies, sooth
    curiosity of the classifieds,
and find some articles of interest.

A Sweet Thought

It's funny, because you might think that the hole you're in is deep, blacker than ink, and so cold. But the sun shows, giving a visual of how far away you are from the opening. Perspectively speaking, the farther something is the smaller it will appear. The hole, with the sunlight, is rather large.

"It makes so much sense," you say, "that the closer something is, the bigger it will appear." This epiphany stirs up such an excitement that you spring upward, off your ass and finally on your feet — your toes actually, since you're so rejuvenated by the sunlight.

The extra leverage of your toes is unnecessary, for already you stand so tall. Enough to mimic a groundhog, surfacing its head to check for spring. And only the head. Raise your arms, fully extend them. Bent elbows mean surrender. Your hands, equitable — naturally curved. Let all, not one, be raised. Your strength will pull you out, it has to.

You move your arms, not to surrender or single yourself out, but to be able to find a grip above the hole. Notice how heavenly the grass feels. The dirt is dry and dusty, meaning it is warm. Let its warmth motivate you. Tired of this hole and want a new one? Let that want get you out of this current hole. Jump, pull, stretch, reach, dig. Do what you need to get out.

"To get out," you heave a large breath, just as you heave your body up. "I need to do what I need to do."

You do it, you get out! (How long did it take? Did you count? Not that you need to, unless you want to. Climb and count. Time is just a conception. Yes, raise your concern of every rising moon and setting sun — how many times has the Big Dipper turned? When do the leaves bud and pop from wintery, naked branches? When do they cut themselves off and die? How long did it take?)

You did it, you got out. Climbing and counting in your own subjective way. Everything has one layer of sunlight on it. The warmth makes you realize just how cold you really are. It's harrowing because you're so cold. Your skin rises along your limbs and your nose red and feels like an ice cube. The sun will warm you and, eventually, the hole.

Your structure, or lack thereof, of time passes. The sunlight hasn't budged but the power source has; it has moved closer to the direction we call "west."

"I feel …" Your words discontinue from your thoughts, right now too exhausted to continue the action of moving your lips and the art of rounding your tongue into words. But you follow up anyway. "… like a muffin."

Uplifted, expanded, and warm. What muffin you are is up for you to debate. Preferably one that just came out of the oven, after being beaten together in a bowl by a spoon, separated, and placed, bit by bit, on a baking sheet. (Yes, you have become baked.)

It's not the warmth that makes you feel like a muffin, it's the sweetness. Whether it be from the sugar or butter, pinches of cinnamon or chocolate — raisins, pecans, frosting — the sweetness of a muffin is what you feel. Within you is just sweet. The sun, the openness of your new surroundings, the familiarity of the environment, the sweat from being too warm, the sleep, the room your arms and legs have, your own constitution of time. Whatever it is, you feel like a muffin, and it's so sweet.

Nicole Tolman

Nicole Toma-Tolman aspired to be an author since 3rd grade, when she wrote and illustrated her first chapter book called The Heroic Magical Monster, followed by several others through her early years. Soon after that, she discovered the thrill of being published (in school and local papers, and a scholastic composition manual) and further studied English and Creative Writing in college. Soon after, she began writing novels and, once upon a time, questions and short informational articles for quizzclub.com. She is a member of the National Association of Professional Women, the Association of Writers & Writing Programs, and the Fox Valley Writer's Group. She regularly attends writers' conferences and events, eager to continue learning more about her coveted occupation.

When she's not writing, she can be found doing charity work, taking care of her husband and three kiddos, baking (she is dangerous with a spatula, but hardly ever sets off the smoke detectors anymore), and playing the piano (badly). And, of course, she's always working on her next novel!

Adventures in ?-Sitting

"Taylor, please stay with me," Tyler Maverick said in his most authoritative tone to his twin sister, who was pulling ahead for the ninth time. "We don't know anything about this place except that there is something weird going on."

"I know, right?" Taylor said, spinning to face him, clenching her fists excitedly. She gestured around the empty, abandoned square of Silvercrest Village. "This place was crawling with people not even ten minutes ago! Then, at eight sharp, *bam!* Gone! What is their deal here? Do you think there's some kind of curfew around here or something? Or…" Her eyes shone with excitement. "…do you think they know something we don't? Like, that something bad is about to happen?"

Tyler rolled his amber eyes. "More like this village is full of neurotic nut-jobs that need to exit the 1800's and join us in the present."

He looked disapprovingly at the tiny post office, the ancient town hall, and the elementary, junior high, and high schools situated in a broken circle around the square. His eyes lingered for a few extra seconds on the large fountain in the center of everything that showcased a big statue with a man on a horse, wielding a long dagger and wearing a hooded cloak with a mask over his nose and mouth.

"It's more likely," he went on, "that it's some ridiculous superstition that suddenly made everyone rush home. Maybe they think it's unlucky to be out after dark."

Taylor sighed. "Do you have to suck the fun out of *everything?* Lighten up and enjoy yourself; this is supposed to be a vacation."

Tyler scoffed. "Some vacation! We're in Utah, halfway across the country from Illinois, where it's actually normal, and stuck in a miniscule village in the practically uninhabitable Henry Mountains with no cell phone reception or Wi-Fi whatsoever, and nothing to do or see for many miles except a bunch of glorified boulders in boring Goblin Valley. And you're saying we can actually enjoy it here in this hellhole? My ass! Look around you, this place is pathetic! These people don't even have cars!"

"I saw a garage next to the bus station when we pulled in," Taylor pointed out, perching on the fountain's edge. "There were a ton of vehicles parked there, probably for commuting. The streets of this village are too narrow to drive or park cars, and everything here is within walking distance, anyway. And there is too stuff to do." She pointed to the stables a short distance away that rented out horses for a nominal fee.

"Oh, yeah," Tyler snorted. "Nothing funner than bruising your crack on a temperamental jackass that probably hates this place and the idiots herein even more than me." He kicked at one of the hexagonal bricks that paved the old-fashioned streets of Silvercrest. "Seriously, I can't wait to lay out that gay asshole from Mom's work who recommended this place to her."

Taylor tossed back her sandy-blonde hair and laughed. "That 'gay asshole' works out, like, twice a day. He can pop your head like a zit."

"Pfft, that fairy-deluxe? He can die trying! Anyway, it's getting dark fast. We better get back to the inn."

Taylor reluctantly hopped down from the rim of the fountain. As Tyler protectively grabbed her hand and led her away, she eyed the small, two-story building that served as the high school. With its two strange towers toward the back, the two large white stone gargoyles "guarding" its ebony double-doors, and the tall walls to its left surrounding what must be a courtyard or garden, the school's dark air of mystery seemed to beckon to her. She pensively wondered what it must be like to attend such an awesome-looking school in such a cool little village.

Suddenly, Tyler froze. He pulled Taylor closer to him and turned his head a bit, listening. After a moment, Taylor heard it, too. A rhythmic, patting sound that grew louder with each passing second. It sounded almost like marching… like several pairs of marching feet.

Tyler assumed a puzzled frown. "What the f—? Come on, Taylor!"

He pulled her along into a jog, glancing behind frequently to try and get a glance of the source of the sound. But by now, it was too dark and, aside from the well-lit town square, there were very few lamps dotted along Main Street.

"Ouch! Tyler, quit yanking me!" Taylor hissed as he took a sharp right down a narrow side street.

"Then keep up!" he snapped. "One… two… three… four… five… six." Tyler halted in front of the sixth house on their right and frowned. "Wait, what?"

He cursed and reached into his back pocket, pulling out and unfolding a small map of the town. He studied it for a second before growling, "What the hell? The inn should be right here, remember? But this isn't the right house; the sign out front and the rocking chair on the porch are missing."

"That's because this is the wrong street," Taylor stated nonchalantly, rocking on her heels. "We passed the right one just before turning down here."

Tyler scowled at her. "Why didn't you *say* something, then?"

"Because you know it *all*, Tyler; you wouldn't have listened. And anyway, I wanted to see what was down *this* street."

"A dead end, just like every other street in this lame place!" Tyler shouted in exasperation.

Suddenly, a door behind them burst open, causing Taylor to shriek and Tyler to automatically close his arms around her.

They turned with a jerk to see a rather short, middle-aged man with thick black glasses and thinning grey hair that brushed the collar of his shirt silhouetted in a doorway across the street. He stepped out quickly and slammed the door shut. Through a window by the door, the twins could see a massive stack of mail on a desk inside slowly tilt and tumble out of sight with an audible whooshing sound.

The man hunched his shoulders. "Damn," he muttered.

It was then that he glanced up and noticed the two teens staring. "Who the hell are you?" he queried.

Before Tyler could tell him that it was none of his business, he held up a hand. "Never mind, I don't care. You look somewhat pubescent, so I have a job for you if you'll take it."

"No," said Tyler.

"What kind of a job?" asked Taylor.

"A babysitting job tha—"

"Forget it," Tyler cut in, pulling Taylor's arm. "We hate kids."

Taylor jerked her arm away. "No, *we* don't, *you* do. You hate everybody." Turning to the man, she asked, "So, what's the little one like?"

The man looked thoughtful. "Well, he's male... cute, cuddly, and has been known to be ferocious at times... immensely intelligent and incredibly, uh, gifted."

Taylor smiled. "Ferocious, huh? I bet I could get through to him. How old is he?"

"Hmm... somewhere in his twenties, I believe, but I could be wrong—"

Tyler made a face. "You want us to babysit a cute, cuddly, ferocious *adult?* What, is he a retard or something?"

"Tyler!" Taylor snapped.

"Of course not. I told you, he's very intelligent, which could present a problem. But as long as you keep him in his cage, he should be—"

"That's it, we're out of here," Tyler said flatly, turning to go. "Come *on*, Taylor."

"Well, that's a shame," the man sang. "I guess these four twenty-dollar bills will have to continue sitting in my pocket, sad and lonely without two frivolous teenagers to spend them."

Taylor perked up. "Forty dollars each? Tyler—"

Tyler paused and rolled his eyes. "No."

Taylor crossed her arms. "Fine, leave then. But I'm staying. I want souvenir money."

"Souvenirs? From where? This place has zero gift shops; there's only a dinky little drugstore on the other side of Main Street!"

"It sells keychains, and I want one."

"And what about Mom? You think she's going to just let us

babysit for some random weirdo we met after dark?"

Taylor turned to the man. "Do you have a phone?"

The man distractedly glanced toward Main Street, where the sound of marching feet grew steadily louder. "Somewhere on my desk. I haven't used it in years, so you may have to excavate a bit to find it."

Taylor nodded and turned to Tyler. "We'll just call the inn and let Mom know where we are. She'll be fine, trust me. No psycho on Earth is scarier than you, and she knows it."

"Great," said the man, rubbing his hands together. "There's a snack on the table inside the door for him. You can let yourselves in; I need to shove off."

"Uh-uh," said Tyler, holding out a hand. "Money first."

As he thrust some bills into her brother's palm, Taylor's eyes widened. "Uh, Mr.—"

"Wilman," the man gruffed, closing his wallet.

"Mr. Wilman, are those friends of yours?" Taylor inquired, pointing down the road.

The man and Tyler glanced toward Main Street, where two single-file rows of tall people in cloaks could just barely be seen in the dim lighting, standing still. As if waiting for something.

Almost immediately, an additional figure slid into view at the head of the little side road. Taylor gasped softly as a porchlight washed over him. Like the others in the now still procession, he was shrouded in a long, hooded cloak. A mask could also be seen concealing the lower half of his face.

He looks just like that statue from the fountain in the square! Taylor realized.

As the stranger stared with dark, stern eyes toward the group, Tyler slid his hand into Taylor's and gave it a reassuring squeeze, his eyes never leaving the masked stranger.

The man raised a hand and beckoned toward them.

"There's my ride," Mr. Wilman murmured, rushing toward him.

"Hey, when will you be back?" Tyler called.

"Don't know! Good luck!"

The twins watched as Mr. Wilman rushed into the darkness of Main Street. The air was filled once more with the sound of feet hitting the pavement, rapidly this time, as the lines of cloaked individuals turned and sprinted after him.

83

After a moment of bewildered silence, Taylor said, "Well… shall we?"

Tyler sighed in annoyance and pinched the bridge of his nose. "Whatever. But I'm telling you now, if this dude's wearing a diaper, we're out of here."

"Deal."

The siblings entered the dim house almost apprehensively. Besides the overwhelming scent of stale incense and obvious Seventies décor of green and orange set off by shag carpeting and wood paneling, the house seemed like a typical bachelor pad, right down to the enormous pile of festering dishes in the sink.

As Taylor knelt to tidy up the avalanche of mail, Tyler managed to uncover a phone underneath a foot of newspapers on the far corner of the large oak desk. After looking up the number for Black Cat Inn in his cell's contacts and brushing a spider off the old phone's dial pad, he dialed the inn on the landline and told Mrs. Maverick where they were.

Just as he was hanging up, Tyler heard a shriek. He cursed and rushed to Taylor's side, knocking over the newly stacked pile of mail on the way.

"What happened? What's the matter?" he asked frantically.

Taylor pointed to a small cage with a large rat in it. "Is *that* what we're sitting for?" she squeaked, cringing.

Tyler relaxed a bit. "A twenty-something-year-old rat? I doubt it."

He reached over and plucked a sticky note from the side of the cage. Taylor leaned over to look. It simply read: "SNACK."

Taylor sounded a note of alarm. "This guy feeds his kid *rats*?!"

Tyler narrowed his eyes suspiciously and slowly scanned the room. His eyes fastened on a dark corner that contained furniture with a large white sheet over it. Tossing the note aside, he strode over to the corner and whipped the sheet off.

He stared for a moment before smirking. "Now *that* makes more sense."

Taylor gasped and hurried to join her brother. "Oh my God, he's *gorgeous!*" she squealed.

A massive snowy owl within an enormous wire cage peeked an eye open. At the sight of the strangers before him, he spread his wings and let loose a toe-curling screech.

Taylor yelped and jumped behind her brother. "It wants to eat my face!" she cried, clinging to his hoodie.

Tyler smiled and rolled his eyes. "We just surprised it. Want to hand me that rat? I kind of want to watch it eat."

Taylor smacked his shoulder. "No! We are not going to send a live animal in there to be murdered! Wilman will have to feed his pet himself."

The twins' eyes turned back on the owl as they heard an unhappy growl. The owl was now dangling from his perch by one leg, which was enclosed in a silver cuff with a black stone inset. The cuff was attached to the perch by a thin, sturdy silver chain.

Tyler gave a short laugh. "Serves you right, you dumb bird. We oughtta leave you like that."

The owl growled and jerked around, its immense wings beating the sides of the cage. Its glowing yellow eyes seemed to glower at the pair.

"Tyler, quit teasing him!" Taylor scolded. She peered into the cage, leaning in close. "It looks like his right wing is injured. See that wound on the inside?" She bit her lip for a second, then announced, "I'm going to help him."

Tyler watched warily as Taylor opened the cage. She reached in cautiously.

"Hold on!" Tyler said, pulling her back. "Didn't Wilman say that thing is ferocious? You'd better let me..."

As he reached in, however, the owl screeched and jerked in protest.

Taylor laughed as Tyler cursed and jumped back. "I don't think he likes you, Ty. *You'd* better let *me*."

The owl was still, but wary, as Taylor leaned into the cage and carefully unfastened his bond with some difficulty.

Tyler watched, his expression thoughtful. "Wilman must have a thing for shiny black stones," he remarked.

"What do you mean?" Taylor asked distractedly, helping the owl step back onto his perch. He purred and nipped lightly at her finger.

"As he was running off to join those freaks out on the main road, I saw a leather sheath dangling from the back of his belt. It had a crazy-looking knife in it with a large black stone set into the hilt. The stone on that bird's cuff looks just like it, only smaller."

The white owl allowed Taylor to stroke his head softly before she latched the cage once more. "Well," she said, straightening up and looking around in abhorrence, "it's obvious the guy has... *distinct* taste. I'd say black jewels are a step up from his tastes in interior design."

Tyler smirked. "Yeah, same goes for his selection of incense. It smells like ass in here," he muttered, opening the window by the desk.

As Taylor began to wash the gigantic mounds of dishes in and around the kitchen sink, Tyler resigned himself to mail duty. As he scooped up envelopes, he studied the name on the mail.

Gabriel Wilman, huh? he mused. *He looks more like a Paul, or John... or Gaylord.....*

Upon finishing, he joined Taylor and picked up a dish towel laying on the counter.

"Is that clean?" Taylor asked.

"Who cares?" he shrugged, drying a pan. "You know, you don't have to do the dishes; that wasn't part of the agreement."

"I know," said Taylor, scrubbing at a mysterious substance stuck to a plate, "but watching that owl is so easy, I feel like we're ripping Mr. Wilman off. And besides, don't you think it's kind of sweet that he rescued that owl?"

Tyler snorted. "What makes you so sure he rescued it? Remember the dagger? He's probably a hunter... or a poacher. Those people he took off with were probably his hunting buddies."

Taylor clicked her tongue. "You're always so prepared to believe the worst about people. Think about it, if he *is* a hunter, that owl would be stuffed. But look at him, he's perfectly—"

She turned to glance toward the living room and gasped, dropping and shattering a coffee cup.

Tyler tensed and whipped around. "What?"

Taylor threw the scouring pad she held aimlessly behind her and rushed to the cage in the living room... which now stood empty.

"Agh, I knew I just saw something white disappear out the window!" she groaned. She rounded on Tyler. "Why the hell did you open the window?!"

"Because Wilman's hippie fumes were making me lightheaded!" Tyler shot back defensively. "The more important question is why didn't you latch the cage properly?"

He stepped forward, studied the securely closed cage door, and frowned. "Correction… the more important question is how did a giant owl get out of a latched cage… without unlatching it?"

Taylor grabbed his hand and pulled him toward the door. "Come on, he can't go far with an injured wing. We have to get him back before he gets hurt."

"Or before Wilman hurts us," Tyler added, exiting the house right behind his sister.

They had only jogged a few yards before Taylor shouted, "There!"

Sure enough, there was the bird, waddling furiously toward Main Street. His head swiveled around at Taylor's voice, his luminescent eyes wide. To the twins' surprise, he flapped his wings and rose off the ground a few feet, disappearing around the corner.

"No! Crap!" Taylor cried, sprinting after him.

"We're about to earn that money," Tyler sighed, following at a jog.

When he caught up to his sister, she stood stationary near the fountain in the square, looking all around. "What's the word?" he asked.

"I don't know, I lost him right around here," she admitted.

It was then that Tyler saw a flash of white behind the fountain's statue. "There's the little shit, up there!" he announced, jumping on-to the fountain's ledge.

"Tyler, be careful," Taylor warned, just before he slipped on the slick marble surface and fell into the shallow basin.

Taylor ran to the fountain. When her brother surfaced, she asked, "Are you okay?"

"Yes, I'm fine," he grumbled. "Only smacked my damn elbow on the bottom."

Taylor broke into a grin. "Good, because that was really funny!"

Before Tyler could retort, a dark, tall mass slowly and smoothly arched up from the water… a mere few feet from where he sat. The twins' eyes followed the thick, patterned, scaly torso upward, and they were horrified to see that it was topped off with the giant trian-gular head of a snake.

They both gaped, petrified, as the serpent surveyed the scene be-fore it. It slowly lowered its head toward Tyler, then flicked its long, whip-like tongue out, almost grazing the tip of his nose. Then, its sol-id yellow eyes intense, it slowly drew back…

Suddenly, Taylor let out a deafening scream, and the serpent's gaze shifted to her cowering form.

"Taylor, get out of here!" Tyler shouted, splashing to his feet.

Ignoring his command, Taylor grabbed his hoodie and pulled as he scrambled over the fountain's rim. The snake redirected its focus once more and hissed as it shot forward, firmly clamping its mouth over Tyler's left foot.

Taylor screamed again, pulling harder. Tyler, bracing himself against his hysterical sister, used his right foot to give the snake a sharp kick to the nostril. The snake recoiled with an angry roar and released Tyler, who plummeted to the ground, almost taking Taylor with him. He quickly stumbled to his feet, and the pair bolted toward the high school and hid beside the garden wall.

Taylor pressed herself as hard as she could against the rough bricks, trembling uncontrollably. "Is it coming? Is it after us?" she whispered.

Tyler dared to peek beyond the towering wall, then stepped out altogether. "It's gone," he said in disbelief. "Where did it go? How did it end up in that fountain in the first place?"

Taylor responded with a gasp. "Tyler, the owl!" she exclaimed, pointing to a nearby rooftop.

The owl, as if knowing it had been exposed, let out a disgruntled hoot and took flight toward the garden wall, smacking into it once before flying over.

"Oh, NO!" Taylor whined. "How in the hell are we going to get in there?"

Tyler bit his lip for a moment, a trait the twins shared when they were deep in thought. Finally, he rolled his eyes yet again. "Give me a boost, Taylor."

"Hmm? Oh... okay. But how are you going to get back over afterward? Especially if you have the——"

"I'll worry about that when the little prick is tied up nice and secure in my hoodie. Speaking of, watch for a knotted-up hoodie vaulting over the wall with an unconscious, owl-sized lump in it."

"Tyler... you better not!"

"Taylor, shut up and give me a boost, will ya?"

Taylor grudgingly locked her hands and knelt.

"Now," Tyler said in a stern tone, "don't try to lift me too fast, Tay. And lift with your legs, not your——"

"Give me your damn foot, Tyler!"

Tyler stepped into her hands. She stifled a grunt as she lifted him to within reach of the top of the ten-foot wall. "Jesus, bro, ease up on the Doritos!" she croaked.

He hooked his fingers over a steel railing just over the top row of bricks and hefted himself up and over. "Whoa… hey, there's a walkway up here that leads to the towers in back of the school!" Tyler called down. "Sweet!"

"Stay focused, and please hurry!" Taylor responded anxiously, glancing toward the square. "Try to remember that a snake the size of the Loch Ness Monster is wandering around the village somewhere!"

Tyler smirked. "Still like it here?"

"Bite me!"

Tyler sobered. "Listen, stay in the shadows, Taylor, and don't make a sound. I'll be quick."

Sure enough, Tyler quickly made for the towers.

Taylor paced nervously, chewing one of her thumbnails down to the quick. As a few minutes passed, she started bouncing on the balls of her feet. *Why don't I hear anything? Where is he? What is he doing?* she wondered, her heart drumming so hard she could feel it in her throat. Guilt quickly set in to mingle with her fear. *He was right about everything—this job, this messed-up village… There is definitely something evil about this place; I can feel it now. If anything happens to one of us, it will be all my fault. Tyler, please hurry back…*

Suddenly, her twin's voice pierced the silence. "Aha! Gotcha, you little f—… AAAAAH!"

Taylor slapped a hand over her mouth to stifle an impulse to call to him, remembering his warning to stay silent.

There was some muffled cursing from within the walls, a faint thump, and all was quiet.

Taylor flattened herself against the wall again, pressing her ear to it.

Nothing. Not even a cricket chirped in the small mountain town.

"Tyler?" Taylor whispered loudly.

Silence.

"Tyler?" she quaked timidly… and felt her throat tighten with tears at the persisting stillness.

"What am I going to do?" she whispered. "I need help!" Raising her voice, she cried, "I need help! Somebody! Hel—"

She cut off as she was jerked back, and a hand clamped over her mouth just before her back met with a firm body.

A voice close to her ear murmured, "You really don't know how to listen, do you?"

Taylor sobbed once into his hand before turning and throwing her arms around her twin. "You're such an asshole," she hiccupped into his shoulder.

He closed his arms around her, then reopened them quickly and stepped back. "Shit, I'm getting blood all over you."

Taylor paled. "What?! What happened?"

He held out a blood-soaked, slightly mangled left hand. "I got attacked—well, truthfully, I attacked myself... with a porcupine the size of a Labrador."

Taylor made a face. "A porcupine? In an enclosed high school courtyard?"

"Exactly. Something really jacked-up is going on here, but I can't quite..."

His voice trailed off, and Taylor snapped into action. "You said you attacked *yourself*. What did you mean by that?" she queried, pulling her shirt off.

Tyler turned his head. "I thought I saw the owl duck behind a big statue. But when I rounded the statue and dove on him, it was a giant porcupine. I got a fist full of quills, stabbed my hand up pretty bad. It ran toward some bushes in the courtyard. I couldn't find the owl."

Taylor tore two long strips from her light blue cotton shirt. "And your other hand? Why are your knuckles all broken open?"

"I got pissed and punched a tree," Tyler admitted, and quickly added, "There goes your bird."

Taylor looked up to see the owl gleefully soar above them. "We'll worry about him in a sec; you're more important now," she said firmly, noting that it had descended into the forest on the edge of town before turning back to Tyler. "How did you get out of the courtyard so quickly?" Taylor asked, wrapping his left hand.

"The door leading into the school cafeteria was all busted up," Tyler shrugged. "I just walked right through it and came out the front. I got lucky."

"For once tonight," Taylor grumbled, tying a knot over Tyler's bloody right knuckles. "Alright, come on; the owl's in that forest just past Wilman's street. Hey!" she objected as Tyler yanked his yet-to-dry hoodie down over her head.

"If Wilman and his freak parade come back tonight, there's no way they're gonna gape at my half-nude sister," Tyler said, adjusting his Sex Pistols T-shirt.

"I'll dress myself next time, thank you," Taylor seethed, patting her hair back into place.

The twins half-heartedly trotted toward the woods, each beginning to wonder if they should really continue on and enter into the unfamiliar mountain wilderness to pursue Wilman's pet. Even at forty bucks each, it was beginning to look like Wilman had ripped *them* off instead of the other way around.

As they entered the alpine forest, Tyler grabbed Taylor's elbow and pulled her close. "Please stay by me. This place freaks me out... *hard.*"

Taylor laughed nervously. "Aw, you need me to hold your hand, too, little bro?" she teased.

But her voice betrayed her nerves. If Tyler was scared, it probably meant she should be terrified.

As they slowly walked into the deathly quiet forest, Taylor whispered, "The trees here are so short. Wouldn't you think these trees would be huge?"

"It's the elevation," Tyler replied, feeling like he should whisper, too. "The higher up you go, the shorter the trees get until they stop growing altogether. The elevation they cut off at is called the timberline. In a climate like Utah, there is usually an upper and lower timberline. Harsh conditions make it practically impossible for trees to grow above a certain point in the mountains, but the arid climate in most parts also makes it hard for trees to grow near the desert floor."

Taylor felt a touch of pride as she nudged Tyler with her shoulder and teased, "You're such a know-it-all."

As they trekked on, the twins gradually became aware of a soft roaring sound and the babble of moving water. Moments later, they came to a small clearing with a trickling mountain brook cutting through it. In the full moon's luminous glow, the twins' identical amber eyes followed the path of the brook upstream until they saw the source of the soft roar: a distant waterfall that spilled into a rippling lake at its base.

"Oh my God, it's beautiful!" Taylor gasped.

Tyler's attention, however, was immediately elsewhere. He jerked back violently, and his sharp intake of breath got Taylor's attention.

"What is it?" she asked fearfully.

She traced his horror-struck stare just in time to see a massive, dark-red animal duck back into the dense lining of shrubs across the brook.

Taylor whimpered shrilly. "T-Tyler——"

Tyler quickly regained his wits and dragged her back into the forest a few feet. He yanked her down behind a large red boulder. Raising a trembling finger to his pale lips, he softly hissed, "Ssshhhh..."

Taylor's face became pinched as tears came. "Was that a lion?" she breathed out shakily. "I saw a mane, and fangs, and glowing yellow eyes, but that couldn't have been a lion, could it?"

Tyler shook his head grimly. "I got a better look than you. That was no lion."

Shimmying his back up the boulder, Tyler dared to peek over the top. He tensed as the familiar form of the white owl clumsily ascended from a treetop and swooped low over the stream, due north.

Tyler scowled, picked up a good-sized rock that lay beside the boulder, and took off toward the owl. Taylor groaned and hesitantly followed him, giving the growth opposite the stream a last apprehensive glance.

She had almost caught up to her brother when he suddenly stopped and took careful aim. She skidded to a halt, almost colliding with him, and eyed the rock warily. "Tyler... what are you doing?"

Tyler grunted as he heaved the rock toward the animal. The rock hit its large, low-flying target easily, bringing it down with a panicked screech.

Taylor shoved him. "Tyler!"

He dashed toward the fallen bird, his gaze fixed and determined. She charged after him, grabbing his shirt before he could dive on the owl.

The injured bird of prey growled at the two, puffing its feathers menacingly.

Taylor took pity on the poor animal. "It's okay; we won't hurt you again, we promise," she cooed gently.

"The hell we won't!" Tyler barked.

He tore away from his sister's grip, grabbed his previous weapon of choice a few feet away, and stomped to the owl, pinning him down with one arm and raising the rock high with his other.

"Enough games, you little bastard!" he spat.

The owl hooted inquiringly.

"Tyler, what the hell?!" Taylor screamed. "Have you *completely* lost it?"

"You've had some rather strange buddies looking out for you tonight, huh bird? Like that abnormally gargantuan reticulated python chilling in the fountain… that is only native to southern Asia! And then there's that freakishly large African porcupine I ran into that somehow made its way into the Henry Mountains of North America—"

"Tyler…"

"—and not to mention the nifty little mythological chimaera you managed to conjure up. How do you explain that?"

"Mythological *what?*" Taylor inquired.

"Chimaera… something the Egyptians concocted. It's said to have the head of a lion, the body of a goat, and the tail of a dragon or scorpion. This particular chimaera had a dragon's tail."

He's flipped! Taylor though wildly. "Tyler, that's not possible," she sighed.

"You're telling me?" Tyler snapped at her. He turned back to the owl and waved the rock threateningly. "Show yourself, right *now*, asshole!"

Taylor bit her lip, desperately trying to think of a way to snap her brother out of it, when suddenly, with an exclamation of surprise, Tyler shot upright of his own will. He backed up defensively into Taylor, who curiously leaned to peer around him. Her eyes grew wide… and she whimpered in terror.

The owl was bubbling and swelling, shifting and twitching. Its legs extended and thickened. Its wings lifted and lengthened, the downy tips taking on the distinct shape of human fingers. The silky white feathers on his body sank and flattened into white garments, while the feathers on his head grew out and flowed downward, climbing down a rapidly forming, slender male torso like ivy.

Before Taylor's numb mind could catch up with her eyes, there was a fully formed man, wearing what appeared to be a gi with a gold belt, weakly kneeling before them on his hands and knees, his long white hair cascading down over his face and sweeping the ground beneath him.

Taylor stepped out from behind Tyler, her head still buzzing with disbelief. *Mr. Wilman's pet is an old wizard,* she realized, her lips twitching up into a dazed half-smile. *I wonder if he knows…*

Tyler glared down at the man, his fingers still clutching his rock tightly. "Get up," he said, his tone low and sinister.

The man slowly and obediently rose.

Upon a quick and thorough survey, the first thing Taylor noticed was that he was tall… taller than Tyler. She also noticed with wonder that his face did not appear to be old at all. She guessed that he was maybe in his mid-twenties. He also had a red, bloody tear in his attire, up by his right shoulder.

He looks tired… and weak, Taylor thought, biting her lip. *And… scared? Of Tyler?*

The man stood rigid and still, his eyes cast down and his hair shining with a silvery brilliance in the moonlight. Taylor continued to study him, suddenly full of questions she was too afraid to ask. She felt puzzled when she realized that what she wanted to know most was his name.

Tyler spoke again. "I knew something was off about your whole innocent owl act. You were every one of those jacked-up animals we ran into tonight. But the rational part of me needs some answers, buddy. Just what are you, some sort of magician? An illusionist?"

The man's lips parted. "No," he said quietly.

"Speak up!" Tyler ordered sharply. "And didn't your mother teach you any manners? Look at me when I'm talking to you!"

The man obediently lifted his gaze, eliciting a gasp from Taylor and causing Tyler to drop his rock.

This man had the most incredible eyes either twin had ever seen. They were a soft gold color, with vivid yellow rings around his pupils that streaked outward through his golden irises like starbursts. The outer edges were starkly outlined in a cinnamon brown.

Taylor exhaled softly. *He is beautiful,* she marveled inwardly, her heart soon beating with a more pleasant quickness.

"No," the man repeated more loudly.

Tyler blinked hard in an attempt to shake off the instant stupidity this man's gaze had inflicted on him. "What are you?"

"*Who* are you?" added Taylor, cringing at the timid and shy way her voice had ridden out.

Her breath halted as the beautiful stranger's amazing eyes fixated on her. She blushed darkly, but held his stare.

"I am Alexei Korsakov," he said, a thick Russian accent permeating his words, "lowly servant to the brethren of the Straydor Dynasty and slave to the Lord of the underground city and his heir."

"S-Slave?" Taylor stammered feebly.

"And I am not a magician," he continued, glancing at Tyler. "There is not magic or illusion behind my ability, only science that is not easy to explain. I would be better described as a shapeshifter."

Tyler scoffed. "Well… of course you are, pal." With this, he knelt down to retrieve his discarded rock and raised it, stepping toward Alexei.

"Tyler, no!" Taylor screamed.

"Hold it there, lad!" a familiar voice called.

The twins whirled around to see Wilman enter the clearing. He strode right past the twins and to Alexei, whom he eyed severely. Waving a particularly ornate dagger under the dejected shapeshifter's nose, he intoned, "Move from this spot and I'll skewer you again, Korsakov."

He tapped the wound on Alexei's shoulder for emphasis.

Taylor frowned and clicked her tongue in disgust. "So, you *do* know!" she accused, glaring at Wilman. "Not only do you and your deranged cult own this man illegally, but you beat and wound him, too? What kind of a sick slave driver are you?"

Wilman raised a brow. "Who?" He jerked his dagger toward Alexei. "That? No, my dear, young Mr. Korsakov is not my slave. He is my prisoner."

Taylor turned to Alexei, who nodded ever so slightly to confirm this. She then narrowed her eyes at Wilman, puzzled. "Okay… why—?"

"Let's just say his master is an old enemy of this village and the monastery that protects it," Wilman explained. "This boy here could lead us to the entrance of his master's hidden city, but despite his mostly subservient manner, he will not offer up the info."

"I will be tortured if I do," Alexei informed him.

"More people will die if you don't," Wilman retorted.

"*You* will die if you find them," Alexei countered.

95

"Wait, what did you mean by 'boy?'" Tyler suddenly interrupted. "This guy has to be, what, thirty?"

"I am twenty," Alexei corrected.

Taylor felt a secret thrill at these words. *Only three years older than me,* she calculated. *Hells yeah!*

"Sure, sure, just let the adults talk, junior," Tyler said dismissively.

Taylor saw Alexei's eyebrows turn ever so slightly down, but Tyler didn't notice.

"So," he said, turning to Wilman, "your dagger looks remarkably like the dagger that the rider from the fountain in the square is holding… the rider that is dressed almost identically to the dudes you ran off to play with." He leaned in, tilting his head facetiously. "Does that mean you're a monk?"

"That, son, is none of your damn business," Wilman answered, jovially cuffing Tyler's shoulder.

As the pair continued their alpha male battle of wits, Taylor worked up the nerve to address Alexei.

"Hey," she said softly, leaning against a stump a few feet from him.

As Alexei's eyes found her once more, she fought to maintain her composure enough to not become a babbling imbecile. "My name is Taylor. The loud and bossy one is my twin brother, Tyler. I hope he isn't scaring you. He pretends to be so tough, but he rarely fights," she lied.

Alexei turned and took a few steps toward her before dropping to his knees at her feet and resting back on his heels. She stared down at him with wide eyes, her stomach fluttering almost painfully. *Is this guy even real?* she wondered, discreetly admiring his unusual features yet again. *He looks like something out of a fantasy novel… or just a fantasy….*

She blushed at the impure thoughts that suddenly materialized in her imagination, but Alexei's velvety voice brought her crashing back to reality as he responded, "My fear has nothing to do with your brother. I fear another, a powerful and cruel being who grows more dangerous to me with each hour I am away."

"Your master?" Taylor guessed.

Alexei nodded slowly.

"He's not good to you, then?"

Alexei bowed his head sorrowfully, and Taylor's heart broke.

Where have you been, Alexei? she silently asked him.

Aloud, she asked, "Why don't you just stay with Wilman, then? If you can give him the info he needs, and even help him and the monks fight, you can bring your master down and—"

She swallowed the last of her words as Alexei shook his head. "As long as I sleep or dream, he will find me. He has complete control of me. If I try to resist, he will do things so horrible, so unbelievably cruel, that they will drive me to madness. My only escape is death."

Taylor shivered. Did someone like that really exist?

Nearby?!

"That is precisely why the Porta-Custodis monks must find and destroy your master," said Wilman, who had stopped arguing with Tyler to listen in. "They are the only ones who possess the knowledge and tools that can defeat him."

Alexei's face hardened. "And if you march into his city soon after my capture and the attack fails, it is on *me*! He will know I talked."

"Don't be a coward, Korsakov; this ancient war is bigger than you and your humble existence."

Alexei's face twisted in pain, then fear, then defeat. "If… If I were to tell you… you must promise to kill me immediately after."

"Done," Wilman promptly concurred.

"No!" Taylor shouted. "You cannot kill Alexei; let him go!"

Mr. Wilman sighed in annoyance. "My dear, with all due respect, butt *out*. The sooner his master is removed from being, the better for everyone… you included."

Taylor arose from her stump and stood stubbornly in front of Alexei.

Tyler snorted. "Oh, here we go," he muttered under his breath.

Taylor pointed behind her at Alexei. "This man is forced against his will to serve a master who torments and abuses him. And now, he has to suffer for the guy's sins, too? That's not fair!"

"Sounds to me, then, like he's better off dead anyway," pointed out Wilman, polishing his dagger with his shirt.

"No," Taylor repeated. "There has to be another way…"

"Why not use Korsakov as a spy?" Tyler offered. "Then you can spare him, he can give you updates on his psycho boss's schemes, and he can give you the location to the city when his boss isn't on his guard."

Mr. Wilman stood silently for a moment. Then, his face began to contort and flex as he mulled this option over.

After a suspensefully long minute or two, he sighed. "The disturbance we were informed about near Goblin Valley... is that your master's doing? A diversion of some sort?"

Alexei lowered his eyes. "Yes. He wove a dream while I slept, ordering me to wait for your departure, find a way to escape, and to come back to him immediately. I told him about your cuff with the monks' stone in it, that I couldn't shift within it. He told me that I had better find a way.

"Upon your leave, I was going to attempt to escape the cuff somehow, and even go so far as to gnaw my leg off if I had to. When I discovered that you hired people to watch over me, I thought all was lost... until I figured out that they didn't know of my true nature."

Alexei glanced at Taylor contritely. "I found a way to trick them into opening my cuff so I could shift into a shrew and escape through the bars. I apologize for abusing your empathy... and for trying to frighten you into giving up your pursuit." Then to Tyler, "I didn't mean to hurt anybody."

Tyler's expression softened slightly. "Whatever, Taylor's shirt looks better on me, anyway," he joked, earning an indignant "Hey!" from his sister. "But next time you're trying not to hurt anybody, don't mimic an animal with quills, genius."

Alexei bowed slightly. "I am sorry."

"Well, now that we're all friends," Wilman spoke up, "let's get back on topic. Korsakov, what are the chances that your master's minions will provoke a battle with the monks tonight?"

"As low as five percent, and that is only if they are somehow forced to. The main function of the diversion is to draw the monks' attention away from my point of entrance, and that includes any of their spies that may be in the vicinity. The master is highly vigilant right now and a battle near a state park and popular tourist attraction may draw even more unwanted attention to the area."

Wilman sighed and shook his balding head despondently. "The monks are going to break my balls for this, but considering the circumstances..." He waved at Alexei. "Get the hell out of my sight. Just remember this...

"I personally know the lad that is to inherit you, your master's 'heir' as you call him. He is a student at the high school here in the village, and I am one of his teachers. I shall keep track of you through him. He is a good lad, so you and the bastard you presently answer to best not screw with him.

"Secondly…" He raised his dagger meaningfully, the moon glinting off its large black stone. "…you feed me any red herrings, you die. Painfully. Do not forget that I own one of the only weapons in the world that even someone like *you* can't heal from."

Alexei nodded shortly, then fastened his gaze on Taylor. She gulped hard as he slowly approached her. When he stood just before her, gazing down at her, his golden eyes unreadable, she guiltily averted her own. "I took away your one escape, didn't I? You wanted to die… didn't you?"

"Not especially," he answered. "There is still much I must do."

"You… Will you be punished… for getting captured by his enemies?"

"Soundly and severely."

Taylor closed her eyes, her lip trembling. "No one… No one should have to endure…" She cut off, too upset to finish.

Alexei placed a slender finger under her chin and guided her gaze back to his. "It is for the better. The master is in love with me and my ability. If I did not return, his wrath would spread like a plague to all corners of the continent. And anyway, I can handle it. I always have."

Alexei leaned in toward her, and for a brief, fervently hopeful moment, Taylor anticipated his lips on hers. Instead, she felt his breath caress her ear…

"Thank you so much for your kindness," he breathed.

Tyler, who had tensed and was frowning darkly during this exchange, reached for Wilman's dagger.

"Hands off my junk, boy," its owner said evenly, and Tyler withdrew his bandaged hand.

Taylor, entranced by the shapeshifter's tenderness, gave a start as Alexei suddenly spun away, dove gracefully into the air and shifted quickly into an owl. He disappeared without delay, weaving away through the trees like a white wind.

"Showoff," Tyler muttered.

Taylor sighed longingly. "He was *so hot!*" she whined.

Tyler made a face. "Taylor, you're not even allowed to date."

She twisted around to glare at him. "Says who?"

"Says me, unless you want your crushes to start mysteriously disappearing."

Wilman replaced his dagger in its scabbard and eyed Taylor solemnly. "Forget him, girl. Trust me; that is not a world you want to be a part of."

Just forget him... easy enough, she thought sarcastically.

"So," said Wilman, clapping his hands, "who wants to join me at my place for some Crap Soup, which I've been told tastes much better than it looks... or smells. Only forty bucks a bowl."

Tyler grimaced. "As appetizing as that sounds, I think Taylor and I should head back to the inn before we run into any more freaks like you and Korsakov."

Wilman shrugged. "Your loss."

The group walked in silence to Black Cat Inn. When they were safely at the door, Wilman gave a quick salute. "Stay alive," he simply said before strolling away, whistling cheerfully.

When Tyler pulled open the front door, they were practically pounced upon by the plump, rosy-cheeked owner of the inn.

"Hello, children, I'm so happy to see—" She gasped. "Why, Taylor... what happened to your hands?"

Tyler rolled his eyes. "It's Tyler, Mrs. Bombay, and I'm fine. Just a few scrapes."

"Oh... I see. Well, I expect you two had fun babysitting?"
Silence.

"Right. Well, how would you like to make a little more money to line your pockets with?"

"We're listening," prompted Tyler.

"Okay, Mr. Maverick, your mother tells me you're a fairly gifted artist. Is that correct?"

"I dabble," Tyler confirmed.

"And Miss Maverick, you can earn your share by simply painting over the sign out front so your brother may have a fresh canvas to work with."

Taylor wrinkled her brow. "You want us to paint over the sign for the inn? But why?"

"I'm renaming it," the innkeeper announced proudly.

Tyler stretched and yawned before nodding in understanding. "It probably *would* be better for business if the name were a bit less ominous." He glanced at Taylor who nodded as well. "Sounds good;

we'll do it. What name do I slap on the sign?"

"Well, see, I was by the window knitting only a short time ago when my inspiration flashed by overhead in the sky. It was a great, big snowy owl! I didn't even know they lived here in Utah!" She sighed. "It was the most beautiful thing I've seen in a long time. So, I am renaming this place White Owl Inn! What do you think?"

To the woman's surprise, Tyler groaned loudly and stalked up the stairs. There was the muffled sound of a door slamming shut seconds later.

The innkeeper looked at Taylor in bewilderment. "Is it really that bad?"

Taylor smiled widely. "Not at all. It sounds wonderful."

Kerry White

Once upon a time in a small village there was born a male child of unusual strength, vitality, incredible handsomeness and intelligence. He lived down the street from where Kerry White was born. This required Kerry to become a thinker and writer of ...thoughts. He constantly strives to find the uncommon, unusual or nothing at all; gazing off into some far away distance before the dinner bell rings. Other days, he is a pirate, for pirates have no bounds and can do anything they want, when they want and however they want to.

Kerry has been published in FewerThan500, Flash Fiction Magazine, Foxtales 2, 3, 4, 5 and most currently in Phantasm's Door.

Shades of Grey

The city was on fire. Concentrated cannon fire still pounded the center of it. Pockets of resistance held out hope for assistance while watching ammunition dwindle and body counts rise.

Little Sorrel flinched from a loud burst of cannon fire making General Thomas Jackson, nicknamed Stonewall by his troops, reach over the saddle and pat the horse to calm it. *Easy boy, don't want to toss me just now.*

Horse and rider were subjects of mundane appearance; the horse, a scrubby, short legged Morgan and the man medium in height, long unkempt beard and in an undistinguished grey uniform. Both were exceptional in other ways as Jackson had proven to be a tactical genius and the sorrel sturdy and stalwart in battle. His talents and the horse's endurance had brought them each to this battle in the war that had gone on so long.

This is the one. The last and final conflict of this cursed war. I vowed this on Lee's grave and I will not be denied my victory. God be on my side.

Almost two years ago he had been close to death himself; shot accidently by his own men. His recovery was as remarkable as the means; a tea brewed from the purple coneflower, *"A damned daisy for righteous sakes,"* used as a last resort by a field doctor for his pneumonia. His arm, at first thought to need amputation, had also recovered perhaps by the sheer bullish will of the patient. *"Leave my arm or lose your head!"* The doctor learned that day never to cross a God fearing Presbyterian from Virginia.

For days the Washington fighting had been bloody and foul. This last bastion of Northern consolidation was desperate in all respects. Most had fled weeks ago knowing that the Confederacy was but fifty miles out. Months earlier, the Union's two generals, Sherman and Grant had lost their attempts to take the Southern Gateway through Atlanta, Georgia. The assassination of General Robert E. Lee by a Union spy afterwards had bent but not broken the morale of the Confederacy. Stonewall Jackson was the unanimous choice for a successor and had with swift determination turned the seething wrath of his troops towards the North.

Now, at last, Jackson stood poised to have his greatest victory; the White House of Lincoln was surrounded completely. Stonewall re- trieved his binoculars and studied the defenses circled around the building. The land was a scarred, smoke covered hell of craters, dis- membered bodies, horse carcasses and wrecked wagons.

Not long now... His attention was drawn to movement on the roof. A figure raised a long pole with a tattered Union Flag and waved it back and forth in brave defiance. Jackson adjusted his binoculars. The man on the roof was unmistakable; taller than most, black hair and beard, strong, angular features.

It's the devil himself, he thought and turned to his Lieutenant in charge of ordinance. "Fire the cannons at will Lieutenant. Turn it into dust. No mercy."

It's Complicated

It's Complicated

"Summer, then Fall and Winter followed by Spring. We have seen many seasons together, haven't we? I could easily see dying in Spring, Aerill; everything new and growing," The old man said.

Immortal Aerill, the sylph, stretched as feline as possible on the chaise, flashed a pointed smile and sprang to grasp his chest over the heart, fingers extended, claws out and pricking through the tweed garments to his skin. He felt a blood trail drip down from one.

"Oh, let me do it, warlock, a quick death for you and a juicy heart for me," it whispered in sultry tones through luscious lips.

He laid his spotted hand over Aerill's on his chest, "It would be release for you if I agreed, Your binding has been for decades now. Is that what you want?" Its grip sank deeper, then released. He pulled the elemental closer, peered into the moss green eyes before him and placed his mouth over the parted lips. Aerill's snake tongue lashed between them, rough and eager. Her tail reached around between his legs and moved them even more intimately closer.

He broke the moment, "Not yet, my lovely." Aerill pushed him away and returned to the chaise. Eyes dimmed to slits; tail swishing, back and forth.

He reached for his coat and staff, "I have a errand to run." Aerill showed no reaction. "It involves a nasty dragon in Brendenshire. They've asked for my assistance." Still not a twitch.

He opened the door to walk out but paused, "Would you miss me Aerill, if I was gone?" Without looking he knew she had materialized behind him.

Aerill's voice rasped into his left ear, "You are a silly old warlock but you had me at dragon and I am bored and oh, so hungry."

They walked into the brightness of a fine Spring day together.

More Complicated

"It appears there is good news and bad news," the Warlock muttered. Aerill, the spirit - bound, immortal sylph, crouched next to him, sphinx - like. Brendenshire's dragon problem was busy nearby, eating and burning its way through the village. Half of a man's torso lay at the two observers' feet.

"Bad news: the dragon is bigger and more aggressive than the good burgermeister let on." Looking down, he added, "Good news: this is what's left of our fine burgermeister." Aerill sniffed the remains and gave the Warlock a questioning look. "I can tell by his argyle socks." Roars, screams and smoke drifted over the slight, warm breeze reaching them.

Aerill said with a smirk, "Surely he paid up front." The Warlock frowned and shook his head.

"Pro Bono," was his dry reply. He raised his staff, closed his eyes and began to draw the magic in. The breeze turned into a whirlwind around them, picking up leaves, sticks and the errant squealing rodent or two. The air stilled, debris and rodents hung in suspension. The staff thrummed with power. With a forward thrust the Warlock directed all the massive energy towards the dragon; a killing blow. With a cry of pain the Warlock went to one knee just as he released the force, causing it to misdirect. "Damned arthritis!" he yelled.

The sylph chuckled deep in its throat. "Good one, Warlock. You just destroyed the end of its tail." With a howl the dragon turned towards the offensive duo and advanced in their direction. Massive feet made tremors across the earth. "And you got its attention, too, I see." Aerill resumed being sphinx still.

The old Warlock struggled, grunting. "I have fallen and I can't get up." He continued to try but only succeeded in going down on both knees. Aerill opened one slanted eye and looked at his efforts. The dragon was getting much closer. Waves of sulphurous breath reached them. The ground was jumping in unison with dragon legs pounding the earth.

The sylph stretched, twitched its long tail and growled, "Time for lunch. I'll take one for the team, old man." It slapped its tail against the Warlock's butt and started trotting directly towards the dragon. As the sylph increased speed, its body gained bulk and height to almost ten times its normal size. Dodging the dragon's blistering fire, Aerill lept and sank ten inch long, razor sharp claws into its neck.

Impressed, as usual, with such abilities, the Warlock ceased his struggles. *What a marvelous and beautiful creature you are,* he thought. From behind him floated a grey, smoke cloud, smelling of rotten eggs, and the crunching sounds of mastication. Dreading it, he turned to look over his shoulder.

From the other direction he heard Aerill's battle cry; unaware if it was victory or defeat.

Five feet from his kneeling position stood an adolescent dragon starring him in the face; chewing on long leafy greens. *A Vegan dragon, how quaint!*

Complicated Enough

Aerill appeared at his side, claws dripping purple dragon blood, a large hunk of half eaten meat held in one hand. They both now faced the adolescent dragon calmly chewing on long, leafy greens.

"Super tender, free range, too," the sylph said between bites. She moved towards the young dragon. The Warlock's arm shot out and stopped its forward momentum; ending up chest height and on one bloodied breast. Aerill hissed, "I may not be able kill you, old man, with your binding on me but I can still break bones."

He hesitated, considered chancing a quick squeeze, decided against it and removed his arm. "This dragon is off limits."

At that moment the dragon received the full brunt of the heady smell from the meat and blood. Its eyes became as wide as saucers and it ran away in the opposite direction, bellowing from fear. It tried to fly using immature wings, vaulting upwards several feet and coming back down. This occurred three times, taking the dragon several hundred feet away.

"It's a Vegan dragon, Aerill. Most unusual."

"Alright, so it's brain damaged-" the sylph began to say. In the same instant the dragon crashed down to earth on its last vault, nose first, flipped tail over snout and became limp in a cloud of raised dust. "-and immensely clumsy." More dragon meat disappeared in one large bite. Aerill stopped in mid chew and eyed the Warlock. "Do not tell me you're thinking what I think you're thinking," was added out the side of a half filled, full lipped mouth.

He sniffed and straightened his coat, "It could be trainable. The meat eating ones certainly aren't."

Aerill laughed deep and hard, began choking, hacked several times finally sending the offending clot of dragon meat sailing to land at the Warlock's feet with an ugly, wet splat. "See what you made me do? Now you've gone and spoiled my appetite." A handy sylph tail wiped the bloddy mess from pouty, wet lips. The balance of the un-eaten meat hunk followed the hacked mess to the ground.

"In eighty years you've never had a more stupidly human idea. It is obvious you have dementia. Release me and let me end this suffer-ing. I'll make it slow and painful for you but so enjoyable for me. The perfect solution."

He looked at Aerill, the toothy smile, the sort soft fur covering, the clotting purple blood stains. *Such lovely eyes...* "In time you will have your freedom," he said softly.

The sylph tapped his head with a long claw, "Make it soon, old man, before you forget everything and dribble in your porridge. I'm going. I see a long hot bath and a nap in my future."

Aerill strode away, tail swinging, sleek round posterior moving just so.

"I am not demented," he said loud enough to be heard. *Not yet anyway.*

He received an upraised middle claw and tail swish in response.

"Dragons have better temperaments than some beings," he mumbled.

Cave In

I'm not even sure why I'm writing this. It's not me, not what I do. Maybe it is what I've always suspected ever since it all began: I'm not completely sane.

They're gone. All of them. Lost somewhere out there or dead; most of those by my own hands. It started slowly, then built and built until there was no stopping it. I tried. I tried so damn hard until even I had to accept there wasn't any way back. My tricks, my gimmicks and my expertise...once or twice it seemed like there was hope in an effort that had good results...then it all crashed down worse than ever. I haven't seen another living human being in over two years. By living I mean not an insane, murderous, unthinking zombiefied person only lusting to spread more of the disease.

Eight years ago, or was it ten? I don't know anymore. I stopped keeping track at some point. Every day has been like the last or the next or the next. Pushing back on the tsunami with bitter results. He finally did it, made the madness happen out of his own. Maybe I shouldn't talk considering my own tunnel vision. After all, if there hadn't been me would there have been him? When I'm gone the gods can sort it all out and render judgement. I used to be judgement, a force for good or so I thought; now I'm not so sure. Not sure of anything anymore really.

He's still out there - I know it. If I could find him, the smallest of thoughts remains in me that he must have had a counteragent, a way to reverse all this. A magic wand he could bait me with, torment me with, never quite letting me take it. I find signs. Notes left for me to see, scrawlings on the walls, in pencil, crayon, chalk or blood. And his cards, always the playing cards, so I know it's him. I've checked the fingerprints over and over to be sure. Matched the DNA.

What he didn't expect was that they'd turn on him too. I'm sure he expected to be able to control what he had done. That didn't happen, so now he has an audience of one. Me.

I look around in the dim light and shadows. I wonder what it all meant - the toys, computers, the trophies. They surround me, accusing me of failure with their gloom and silence. I don't go upstairs to the house anymore. It's even worse there. Down here I can brood and wait and try to plan.

In slow increments I can feel the night fall outside. It's almost my time once more. Another trip into the city without the light to guide me. No one to turn the switch and illuminate the path.

I will go, as I always have, and hunt in their name, for all of them.

I will find him. I will find the Joker.

I'm Batman.

Powerful Magic

Sebastian Delacorte knew from an early age that he was different and extraordinarily not the same as others. He could produce light with just a snap of his fingers. He also realized that it must be kept a secret from anyone else lest he be singled out for his uniqueness; understanding how people would fear him.

Practicing in private he blossomed and found that it had been only a beginning for his abilities; progressing to conjuring fire, controlling electrical current and onto making weather subject to his will. By the time the time clock of life turned for him to age twenty there seemed to him no end to his possibilities. All of this he kept in deeply detailed journals.

He also felt very alone.

His parents were gone but had left him well off. Deciding there should be someone in his life, he sought out a companion and found Delia. The wooing and eventual marriage went smoothly. Both families came from wealth and the union was blessed with uncommon ease. At first, Sebastian was ecstatic. He had a woman and sexual pleasure which satisfied his emptiness. Delia was a delicate flower, who as time went on, demanded much of Sebastian's money and time. Money meant little to him but his time? He found this aggravating as it kept him from the further pursuit of his own specialness. As the blush wore off the rose of Delia he began to resent her presence in his life.

A year and one day later he told her they would travel abroad and explore the world. She was delighted. They packed up, said goodbye to her family and left. Sebastian waited for several weeks and then made his move. Alone together in a rented villa one night he told her how disgusted he was at her intrusions upon his continued development. She laughed at his claims of power. His response was changing her into a toad.

The next day he wrote the her family of a horrible accident: Delia lost at sea in a terrible storm. His heart was broken, he asserted. He returned home for the memorial service and funeral with the toad. Shortly thereafter he set the small creature loose onto his property by the pond, forgot Delia altogether, and returned to his studies.

Two years later, he concluded once again that he needed a companion in his life. This instance would be better than the first, he assured himself. In short time he found and wed a diminutive and passive woman named Portia. She followed Sebastian's every command and never challenged his authority. In time he also came to realize she was as thick as a brick and tired of her dullness and acquiescence. He found it impossible to improve her wit and suffer her bovine nature.

He concocted another death scenario and soon Portia was added to the pond. It surprised him that Delia was still there by the aura she possessed - a sure sign of his magic.. He had not expected her to live that long. Delia the toad croaked repeatedly and hopped his way. Portia the toad appeared lost in its new circumstances. Sebastian turned away and left the two amphibians to their fates.

Three years passed and Sebastian once more felt the need for female companionship, sure he had the answer to his needs. Traveling outside of his homeland he searched for a young woman capable of being shaped to his designs. His best candidate was fourteen year old Yamani. Once he was satisfied, he purchased the young woman with a large sum of money from her poor, peasant parents and returned home with her. He explained to whoever asked that she was his ward and spent the next several years directing virtually every aspect of the woman's life, chosing her education, her clothes, her hair style, her entrance into society,. She became everything he had wished for and never received from Delia or Portia. Yamani, for her part, found that she deeply cared for the older Sebastian. Such was her nature and nurture.

On the occasion of her nineteenth birthday, she produced light with the snap of her fingers. Sebastian was at once excited and anxious, strongly questioning her on how this had come about. She told him about finding his journals and reading them. Through his writings she had experimented and discovered her own special qualities.

Sebastian's own nature was a different matter. Many days afterwards were spent considering the new situation. He had spent years of time and effort molding this woman into the companion he had sought for so long and now he was confronted with this unexpected change. If Yamani could develop skills equal to his own....

Fearful of losing control, he decided once again to stock the pond. His search for her led him to that exact place. She sat quietly on a rounded granite rock near the pond's edges. Two toads sat by her feet.

She looked at him with tears in her eyes, "Is this what you mean for me, Sebastian? The same life as these two poor creatures?"

"It is as I have decided," he replied standing over her.

"Have you no heart, Sebastian, no feelings of love?"

"I...," he stopped and considered the question. What was love when one could control the elements and eventually seek to be a god? "No, I do not but I have power and magic."

"Then you have nothing," Yamani replied.

"It is enough," he said and cast his spell.

Yamani rebuffed it with a wave of her hand. "Sebastian, I have made myself stronger than you in magic. I knew from your journals this time would come and that I would have to be prepared." He threw spell after spell at her until the air smelled of ozone and sulfur. Yamani turned them all away.

Exhausted, Sebastian stood gasping for air, oily sweat dripped down his face. Magic has a physical price. He said to her, "You have beaten me."

"Oh, Sebastian, you defeated yourself. Love is stronger than magic. If only you had learned that as well."

"Then use your power and make me feel love."

Yamani approached him and placed her hand over his heart. "It is not my magic or yours that can do this, Sebastian. You must learn it for yourself by living. You have spent all this effort on power and not life. I will give you a new chance." She cast a great spell and sent

Sebastian back in time to live his life over but not before removing his magic power and taking it to herself. In turn, she released Delia and Portia from their toad prisons and erased any memories they had from the time of meeting Sebastian onward. She returned them to their respective pasts just moments before he had historically entered into their youthful lives.

Close to exhaustion by then, Yamani made two final spells. She sent herself back in time to when Sebastian was born. Then she created a mystical cocoon for herself allowing her to remain as youthful as she was until twenty years had passed from that time, at which point she would once again age normally.

Drained from all this, her magic used up, Yamani slumped down and fell into a deep sleep.

She awoke. Young Sebastian sat on a rock near the pond, watching her with heavy concern on his face.

"I have been quite worried," he said, "finding you here by my small pond. Are you alright? Should I fetch a doctor?"

Yamani stood and brushed off her dress, "That is not necessary. I am fine. I was out walking and became lost. I simply feel asleep."

"I'm sorry, dear lady, should I know you?" he asked. "I thought I knew everyone around here."

"No, I'm sure you do not know me," she replied, looking at his open face and soft brown eyes.

"It's just that...," he started, flustered, "I...I do not know what I was thinking it seems. I'm Sebastian."

She held out her hand to his, "Yamani," she said. His grip was warm to her chilled fingers.

He looked away then back, "That is a rather nice name, I think. You're cold. Perhaps some food and hot tea is in order and then we can sort all this out. Let me offer you my hospitality. I live alone so I hope that is not a problem. Well, I do have a cat so perhaps I should say almost alone." He said with a wry smile.

Yamani felt her hopes rise, "Yes, yes that would be quite alright."

Sebastian grinned openly and offered her his arm. "I am somewhat confused. In some ways it is almost as if you appeared like magic."

Yamani laughed and Sebastian truly liked the sound of it. "Really? I am certainly not that mysterious looking, am I?"

"No, perhaps not," he said with a side glance, "but I must hear your story, all of it."

"Only after I have heard yours, Sebastian and then we shall see about mine," she replied in a soft and tearful voice.

She

How does a man say goodbye to the only woman he has ever, deeply loved? In what way does he let go of the soft, warm hand, the gentle caress or the eyes deep with love in them? What if she is taken from him in a cruel and demented way? For all of me, I do not know and that is why I write this story as it happened to me, Dr. Franklin Dupont, MD/PSYCH

- - -

Closing the door to my study I turned to Sinclair Porter, my patient and dear, old friend. It was late on a rain filled, exceedingly dreary Tuesday night, punctuated by thunder and bursts of lightning. Somewhat put off by being interrupted in my free hours, psychiatry as my profession doesn't mean I cannot be petty on my own at times. Those thoughts dispersed quickly enough by ensuing events.

He had come to my residence unannounced, insisting we meet. He was particularly disturbed this night, more so than during recent office appointments. That in itself should have been a warning sign to me, for those same sessions had been intense and fraught with heavy emotion. Losing one's wife in such an dreadful manner will do that to anyone.

He and I had met at Harvard, years ago. He went on to be a lawyer and myself, a doctor of the human mind and its eccentricities. Both of us are well off and respected in society at this point into our middle years of life.

He refused an offered drink, gesturing agitatedly with one hand.

"Sinclair, please sit down and we'll talk." Pacing for a bit I waited until he sat The low light in the room came from my green shaded desk lamp. I have usually found this to be more calming to patients although it caused his face to be cast in multiple shadows. I observed the great torment there.

He grasped my hand in what I can only now call a mixture of desperation and fear. "Jessica...I can't see her but the sensations, the feelings are so strong...I...," he stammered.

"Deep breaths, deep breaths. Try to calm yourself. These feelings, these sensations you're having are not unusual, Sinclair." I patted his hand and squeezed it in what I aspired to be a sympathetic way. "Jessica's death was particularly terrible, the abduction, the possible satanic ritual evidence--"

"Franklin, I have felt her touch, smelled her perfume...she is calling to me!"

This was a new development; intriguing, yet within the realm of human response to a terrible ordeal. "When, Sinclair? How does this happen when it occurs?" He drew back and placed both hands over his face as if to hide his feelings, then thrust them towards me in a plaintive move.

"At night, in bed...as I try to get to sleep." The focus in his eyes drifted away and his voice became distant in a hollow, low timber. "I close my eyes, feeling sleep begin and at first I am aware of a change in the air around me; a chill, the sensation of expectation. Then her perfume seeps into the room, curling and spreading throughout until it becomes saturated, only it turns to a fetid reek. This is followed by the touching...caresses over my face and my body...things she knew that would excite me...and then the voice, her voice, is in my mind, calling to me, wanting me, drawing me to it...."

I sat back in my chair, fascinated by his words and disturbed as well in equal amounts. This was a possible advance into psychosis on his part. What had been extreme grief previously was leading to a severe break in reality for him. "Sinclair, how long has this been happening to you?" I tried to remember our last session together, three weeks, a month past?

His eyes returned to me from somewhere else and I could see the sadness he felt, as well as trepidation. "Days ago, five or six. I don't know...I haven't been able to sleep. Franklin, I...am...afraid...to sleep."

I could see my direction of treatment clearly. Psychosis brought on by severe sleep deprivation involving the patient's overwhelming grief. "Sinclair, you must listen to me now, carefully. Your grief is causing your mind to create these perceptions. To you they are real because your mind wants to keep Jessica alive. The more you feel the less you sleep. The less you sleep the greater these illusions become and the more they invade your life. This is something you and I must treat straight away." I stood up and walked around to my desk.

"Yes. Yes, I understand." He looked slightly relieved. "It is just all so real to me, Franklin. So damnably real."

"First, we must ease your sleep situation," I said as I opened a locked drawer in the desk and withdrew a plastic pill container. "I'm going to give you two of these, which you will take tonight. They will provide you with some relief. Then tomorrow we will see what the next steps should be." More thunder and lightning scarred the night outside. This was no time to be sending him home. I made a fateful decision. "I want you to stay the night with us, Sinclair. With the storm, I feel the necessity...my wife certainly will understand. Agreed?"

As tense as he had been, considerable ease settled into his posture, "Thank you, Franklin, I do appreciate your help. I am sorry to be such a burden."

I reassured him, "Nonsense, my friend. Apologies are not necessary. Come, let's get you situated." From there I guided him to the guest room, supplied him with a set of my pajamas and watched as he swallowed the two sleeping pills before slipping under the covers of our four poster, guest bed.

He reached out to me and grasped my arm as I turned to go. "Thank you, Franklin. You are a good friend." I smiled and nodded while touching his arm in return. For a moment, I hesitated to turn out the light. What caused that moment has kept me wondering to this day. What thought, quickly fleeing, made my hand linger there? I looked back at his relaxed form, his eyes closed from the medication taking its effect. Perhaps, this change in him had affected me more than I was willing to consider in the clinical mind I used day to day. There may have been some spark of uncertainty in the rest of me, a primitive inkling of the fear we all have of the unknown and what might happen. In the end I decided tomorrow would be a new day for him and that I would see to it then. As it was, I switched off and closed the door, leaving him alone. I went to explain the matter to my wife. She was most understanding; a doctor's wife must find patience a virtue indeed.

- - -

It was dear Helen who stirred me from my sleep. "Franklin, I hear noises," she whispered.

"What...?" I replied, attempting some wakefulness.

"The guest room, I swear I hear voices coming from the guest room."

I sat up on one arm and listened. She was right. Through the open door to our bedroom came a murmur of sound from the hallway beyond. "Stay here by the phone in case I need you to call for assistance. I will handle this." I glanced at her concerned face in the dim light, loving her and at the same time feeling the responsibility for this intrusion into our lives and home.

At our bedroom doorway I listened again, discerning that it was one voice and not all speech. It was coming from the guest bedroom beyond any doubt. From the small space between the door bottom and hardwood floor glimmered an unearthly, green light. It was a sick glow that caused my skin to crawl and revulsion so strong that I almost turned back, feeling the need to close our bedroom door and hide. It required a stern, mental push for me to cross the short distance to the guest room door and force my fingers around the gilded, metal handle. Sharp, painful, freezing cold emanating from it lanced through my hand and up into my shoulder. Patches of skin, detached from my hand, remained on the metal as I jerked back in shocked reflex. I must has yelled something in surprise. Almost simultaneously a cry of "Franklin?" came from the Helen's direction as well as a louder scream of abject agony through the door in front of me, "Jessica!"

Hand wrapped hastily in my robe, I wrenched the door handle down, shoving the door open. More cries of torment came from the bed and Sinclair. The air was thick with perfume and something else, rancid and revolting. The putrid, green, luminescence surrounded him, pulsating in a ghastly harmony with his body as it twisted and moved in the throes of what I can only describe now as demented, sexual passion. He was half naked, his face contorted in a mask of pain and impossibly aroused beyond normal physical allowances. Immobile from the sight, I could but watch as he turned his eyes towards me, tried to reach out with his right hand beseeching my help. Behind me I heard Helen's voice again call to me.

"Helen, stay back and call 911 now!" I shouted.

Sinclair was not alone.

He was stretched across the bed, writhing but constrained within that demon light. It had coalesced into a filmy, disgusting figure radiating malevolence and evil on a level beyond any human understanding; a figure I had seen before, many times, in a form that had evoked devotion, care and love. The very figure of Jessica Porter.

Now, on top of Sinclair lay the opposite of that gentle soul, a loathsome, misshapen entity devoid of any resemblance to normal reality. It controlled him, rode him, abused him without regard to his response and with every whimper or pain filled cry from him it exalted in ecstatic joy.

I tried to go to him struggling to move. The green-lit face laughed in my direction and I realized my physical restraint was no longer my own. I could not, no matter how hard I pushed, get beyond the threshold to the room rejected by the resistance in the very air itself. Sinclair's cries and the movement of the demonic creature astride him became frantic leading to a climax of brutal intensity.

"Oh my God!" Helen was behind me holding my handgun, her face in the green light twisted in surprise, fear, revulsion.

I pulled the weapon from her hand, "Stand back." Raised in the two handed grip I had been taught, I aimed the muzzle squarely at the pumping figure's mass. For one eternally long second Sinclair and I once more made eye contact. I saw such pain, despair and helplessness. I truly wonder what he may have seen in mine at that final moment. I fired once, twice and then yet again. Sinclair arched his back at the same time the figure in green released a moan that could only have come from the depths of some ghastly Hell, filled with the joined voices of trapped and lost souls. Instantly, all light disappeared, throwing the room in complete, deep, darkness. There was silence broken only by Helen and I breathing. Smoke curled from the gun barrel in my shaking hands.

Time had stopped in those moments, made us statues until Helen's hand wrapped around my arm causing me to start. I managed to fumble at the light switch and it did not work. Helen, ever the clear thinker, released me and opened a drawer in a hallway table close by. Weak light flared from a small flashlight in her hand. As she moved it around I could see flashes of a figure in the guest bed, contorted...unmoving.

The doorbell rang along with a heavy pounding on the front door. My attention was centered on the bedroom scene and nowhere else. "That should be the police. I'll let them in," Helen said, her voice shaking. I said nothing. This was beyond my capability to understand, beyond my professional experience.

One thing I did realize and feel to my greatest shame today: my utter cowardice. Whether Sinclair was alive or not, I was not going to enter into that room alone.

- - -

It took some time for the electricity to be restored with the reset-ting of circuit breakers. A lone policeman had accomplished that; his arrival coincided with that of the EMT's.

"That's quite a story you have there, doctor." Detective Bertran looked up from his notebook, that look on his face that denoted *What a load of bullshit.* Bertran was the older of the two detectives that showed up after the paramedics and lone policeman, who together, had estimated this was beyond their authority or help.

His partner, a slightly younger version of Bertran in the making with his dress and manner, was with Helen in another room. I knew this was a common practice for police: separate interrogations. They both smelled of stale cigarettes and coffee.

"It's the only one I have to tell. I'm not sure I believe it myself. I have files at my office that will help corroborate the fact that I was treating him professionally...and as a friend. Grief counseling."

Bertran checked back in his notes. "Porter. Jessica Porter." His eyes rose up to mine with a surprised look. "The satanic killing in the forest preserve several months ago?"

"One and the same," I replied.

Pointing with his finger the detective said, "This is one pile of crap. We still haven't solved that one and you're claiming this might be tied to that?"

I shook my head, "I only claim that what I have told you is the truth as I know it," not knowing how to meet his eyes.

Bertran gave me a frustrated look. "Stay here." He went into the other room. I heard him talking to his partner and then a third voice entered the conversation. The lead detective's voice rose up and cursed, "You are fucking kidding me!" He stalked back to me and dropped my plastic-wrapped gun heavily on the table between us. A bright-orange evidence tag covered half the package. "How many times did you shoot?"

"Three. Yes, I'm sure of it."

"So where are the bullets, doc? They're not in your friend up there, not in the wall, nowhere in the damn room. There's no blood, nada."

I considered that for several seconds before answering, "That would be a good question for someone much smarter than me, de-

tective. I'm sure Helen can attest to the shots used as well as the empty casings in the revolver."

He looked over his shoulder as his partner walked into the room
and shook his head with a frustrated look.

Bertran turned back to me, pointed his finger at me once more,
frustration straining his voice, "You and your wife are not to leave
town without our consent, you hear? This is not over by any means.
Not by a long shot."

After all was done and Sinclair's poor remains were removed,
Helen and I left the house with packed suitcases, preferring a hotel
room in town to the house. It felt tainted and wrong now to us both.

We never returned to it. How could we?

- - -

The police did question us again later, several times. Our stories
remained the same. News stories were written, read, talked about
and eventually forgotten. I left my practice. I found that I no longer
could inspire myself or my patients. Helen and I moved to a different
state and purchased a small farmette with part of our savings, deciding to make life simple and perhaps busy enough to try and forget
that night and its notoriety.

Bertran called me some months after everything had died down.

"How you doing, doc?"

Wary, I replied, "I am no longer going by that, Bertran. We get
along."

"Listen, I know I was rough on you guys but you have to admit
this whole business is pretty bizarre, right? We didn't find a thing to
make a case against you guys and I, uh...don't think at this point we
ever will. You're off the hook and our radar."

"That's good to hear considering we never did anything to harm
Sinclair."

"Kinda hard to prove anything with the forensic evidence. Cause
of death: a burst heart and every bone in his body broken with no
external signs of trauma." His voice changed tone, lower, "Then
there are the other things..."

"Care to tell me?" I heard sounds in the back ground now, bar
sounds, laughter.

"Stuff the press never heard about. DNA, doc, DNA for one.
The M.E. found traces of vaginal fluid on the corpse and the sheets.
We exhumed Jessica Porter's body all very quiet and hush-hush to

get samples. Seems it was a perfect match only green in color."
There was silence between us for a few seconds. A tremor entered his
voice with some slurring of words, "And this, I swear to God, Doc," I
heard a glass slam down, "we also found three bullet holes in her
corpse, two in the left side of the chest and one in the skull. All post-
mortem. The extracted bullets match your gun...it's still in evidence
but don't expect it back--"

"I don't want it, ever," I said firmly.

"The last thing...," his voice lapsed into a cold, raspy whisper,
and for a moment, I felt as if I was starring into that damned guest
room once more, facing Sinclair's twisted body, "The morgue assistant...she was prepping her for reburial...she noticed...she found her
abdomen extended, Doc. They opened her up...I was there and I
wish to heaven I hadn't been. I don't know if I can..." Silence, then
"It...it was this misshapen...dreadful thing, Doc. A baby..." he was
crying now. "It...was...alive...they had to..." His words drifted into a
low moan that I will never forget to my dying day. It continued for
what seemed like eternity. My hands shook, barely holding onto the
receiver.

"Be careful out there, doc," he said in one tortured gasp of air
and then the line disconnected to the sound of a long, droning, elec-
tronic hum.

Cover Artist: Daniel Groenhof

I am Daniel Kenneth Groenhof, Born and raised in the small town of Warrenville, Illinois. My interest in photography started at a very early age; on family vacations I would always have a camera or video camera on me at any given time.

Years passed and not much has changed, going through school I took any and every class I could, eventually taking it as my major in college.

For college I went to College of Dupage, while working part time I worked on getting my degree taking a handful of years to get my associates.

I would have to say college was the biggest help for my photography, learning the discipline and organizational skills that my high school never gave me.

Now I am waiting to see where the roller coaster of life takes me day to day.

Facebook.com/DanielKGroenhofPhotography

Instagram: groenhofphotography

Made in the USA
Lexington, KY
23 December 2017